HOBKIN

HOBKIN

Peni R. Griffin

MARGARET K. McELDERRY BOOKS
New York

Maxwell Macmillan Canada
Toronto

Maxwell Macmillan International
New York   Oxford   Singapore   Sydney

To Michael, the gnome

Margaret K. McElderry Books
Macmillan Publishing Company
866 Third Avenue
New York, NY 10022

Maxwell Macmillan Canada, Inc.
1200 Eglinton Avenue East
Suite 200
Don Mills, Ontario M3C 3N1

Macmillan Publishing Company is part of the
Maxwell Communication Group of Companies.
First edition
Printed in the United States of America
10 9 8 7 6 5 4 3 2 1
The text of this book is set in 12 pt. Bodoni.
Designed by Nancy B. Williams

Library of Congress Cataloging-in-Publication Data
Griffin, Peni R.
Hobkin / Peni R. Griffin. — 1st ed.   p.   cm.
Summary: Two sisters run away from their abusive stepfather and settle in an abandoned house in West Texas, only to find that they are not alone but share the premises with the mysterious and helpful Hobkin.
ISBN 0-689-50539-6
[1. Runaways—Fiction.   2. Sisters—Fiction.
3. Fairies—Fiction.]   I. Title.
PZ7.G88136Ho   1992   91-24079
[Fic]—dc20

Contents

1

The Stark Place

Liza—Liza—Liza—that was her name now. She repeated it to herself several times every hour so as not to forget. Liza Franklin and her sister, Kay, who had the documents to prove it.

Beyond the gray-tinted bus windows, West Texas was as flat as the book of word-find puzzles in her lap; oil wells, cattle, sheep, and buzzards appearing so regularly they hardly counted as varying the endless miles of scrub and barbed wire. Hitchhiking through the Texas Hill Country had been neat; but since boarding the bus in Junction, running away had gotten boring.

"I'm getting a headache," said Liza, "and I'm hungry. When we going to stop?"

Kay had been staring out the window. "I don't know," she said tiredly. "A town's coming up. We just passed a sign."

"Is it one we ever heard of?"

"No. But we've stopped in a lot of towns we never heard of."

"Can I have a candy bar if we don't stop?"

"I guess so." Kay shifted her shoulders restlessly and scratched the base of her neck. She had gotten a new—Liza thought, an ugly—haircut before leaving, and the loose hairs that would not brush off still itched.

Liza tried to work one of her word-find puzzles, but they had begun to seem pointless. Through the bus's huge front window she could see houses and even trees, but they sat on the horizon for a long time. She yawned, and fidgeted, and cracked her knuckles. Time to play twenty questions again. "Hey, Kay. I see something green."

"Is it bigger than a breadbox?" asked Kay mechanically.

By the time Kay guessed that Liza meant the green patches on the bus seats, they were passing a sign that read BRITT, POP. 539, then a graveyard, then a couple of mailboxes marking an opening in thick mesquite. Then the bus turned. It pulled up at an old-fashioned gas station with a long, low addition on the side and the words ICE, BEER, GROCERIES painted in faded red on the part that stuck up past the roof. Just down the highway was a farmers' co-op with a sun-bleached sign, and a couple of mobile homes. The driver's distorted voice over the microphone informed them that this was Britt, and they would be here about fifteen minutes.

Liza started to leap up, but Kay stopped her until most of the others had gotten off. "I think we should stay here tonight," she said quietly, getting their backpacks from the overhead racks. "We can camp out."

"Good," said Liza, strapping into her pack. "Are we going to have a cookout and everything? That'll take a long time."

"Yeah, yeah." Kay, taking the hint, dug a slightly malformed Snickers bar out of the side pocket of her pack and handed it over. "Don't talk so loud. We don't want to attract attention."

The dry heat beyond the bus and the stink of diesel, on top of the long ride and the excitement of the last couple of days, were unsettling to the stomach. Liza bolted the candy, anyway, while they waited in line for the rest room; lunch had been a long time ago. Although the space was cramped, they went into the rest room together and made as much use of the indoor plumbing as they could, even brushing their teeth. Kay made sure their canteens were full and stole some paper towels. "Don't take any notice of anybody," she instructed. "We'll slip off quietly and find us a campsite."

"Are we criminals?" asked Liza hopefully.

Kay paused with her hand on the rest room door-knob. "Where'd you get that idea?"

"You keep telling me to act so secret. And it's against the law to have a fake ID. Mary Alice said so."

"What'd you tell Mary Alice?" Kay demanded, suddenly fierce.

Liza stepped back. "Nothing. We were just talking, and she said so." She felt a little mean when she thought about leaving her best friend the way she had; but Kay had been emphatic about secrecy, and Liza had kept the secret faithfully.

"Mary Alice doesn't know anything about fake ID. It's just that what we're doing isn't anybody's business. You don't want us sent back, do you?"

"Of course not." Liza gave the answer she knew Kay wanted.

"Then you do as I say, and let me worry about what's legal."

They walked out, past the counter where a Mexican man sold cigarettes to a bus passenger, past the microwave where another passenger heated a sandwich, past the Coke machine, the gas pumps, and the bus. The driver unloaded a large cardboard box from the luggage compartment. Kay led Liza across the broad, empty highway.

In the west the sky was electric blue splotched with vivid orange and pink, but they headed away from this spectacle, walking along the shoulder toward the mesquite they had passed coming in. What had taken only a moment on the bus made a long walk, and Liza's mouth dried up more with every step. She was glad they'd stopped hitchhiking. Not one car was in sight on the highway here, and they had passed fewer and fewer as they went west. Liza was glad of this proof that Kay knew what she was doing.

The side road had no gate, just a cattle guard. One shiny aluminum mailbox stood up by the highway: BURGER, said the black and gold letters on the side. Another mailbox leaned rustily against the barbed wire fence, its door dangling. The painted name STARK was dim, but legible. "If we're lucky, that Stark place will be abandoned," said Kay.

"Won't the Burgers see us?" asked Liza, turning obediently.

"Ranches are always miles off the road. Keep your ears open. There might be rattlesnakes."

Hastily Liza, who had been peering into the mesquite shade in search of armadillos, corrected her course and followed Kay straight up the middle of the road. White puffs of dust lifted silently around their tennis shoes, and the wind blew straggles of hair from Liza's braids into her face. Birds carried on their evening conversations, invisible. What with her braids, her pack, and the oncoming dusk, Liza felt pioneery and adventurous. It was a shame they had no horses. This was horse country, not walking country. Maybe Kay could get a job on a ranch, and Liza could learn to ride and grow up to be a champion barrel racer, and she would go back to San Antonio with the rodeo and Mom and her stepfather, Lee, would be there and—

"Earth to Liza," said Kay loudly, to get her attention. "Let's try this road."

"What road?"

"This one," said Kay impatiently. "Watch the thorns."

Now that it was pointed out to her, Liza saw it all right—an opening barely wide enough for one car to get through the mesquite and prickly pear. Judging from the length of the grass between the ruts, no one bothered very often. The scrub on either hand cut their view down to the nearest tree trunks; but before Liza had time to enjoy being in a dark, mysterious tunnel, it ended, and they had reached the abandoned farm Kay hoped for.

There was a windmill, and a barn, and a low gray house with a gallery across the front. The windmill did not turn, and the unbroken windows opening onto the gallery were blankly curtainless. Rust streaked the tin roof, but Liza saw only one smallish hole in it. It looked wonderfully pioneery. "Oh, wow," said Liza, running forward. "Can we stay in there?"

"Hold on," cautioned Kay. "There might be skunks or something. Let me go first."

"I'm not going to bother any old skunks," complained Liza.

"Not on purpose. And the floor might be rotten."

"I bet it's a dirt floor, like the gallery."

Kay led the way between the cedar poles propping up the gallery roof and opened the door. "Shows what you know," she said, stepping up onto a bare board floor. "Don't push. It seems solid enough, but let me check it out."

Liza crowded in after her. The sunset light from the long window in the opposite wall showed them a kitchen. The floor was drifted with dust and pollen, cobwebs waved plentifully in the draft from the door, and the white porcelain of the gas stove and the sink were streaked with reddish brown; but the air smelled relatively fresh, and nothing scurried in the walls. When Kay stamped her foot experimentally, the floor shuddered only slightly. "Oh, hey, there's a wood stove!" she said, going to the potbellied shape under one front window and opening the grate. "It'll be a lot safer to cook on this than on a campfire."

Liza went to the cabinetlike piece of furniture under the other front window and was disappointed to find only two empty, metal-lined compartments. She looked into the next room. Well-lit from windows all around the outer walls, this was the same size as the kitchen and contained stacks of paper and a small organ. "Ooh, look!" she exclaimed, running to pump it; but all she produced was a wheeze and a cloud of dust and moth wings.

"Stop running ahead of me!" said Kay sharply. "There might be tarantulas, or rats, or anything."

"Don't be such a slowpoke, then! You think this used to be a church?"

"It's way too small. Regular people used to have organs all the time, back before radio." Kay opened a window with little effort. "Both these rooms are in great shape. We'll have to be real careful not to hurt anything." The window slid back down with a startling bang when she let go.

On the other side of the kitchen was an empty room with peeling blue-rose wallpaper. Another room had been tacked on in back of that—Liza knew it had been tacked on, because she could tell where a window had been between them, and the back room was higher. Kay explored a tiny, windowless bathroom with the flashlight. The toilet stood open and waterless, and a couple of large washtubs, one with a wringer, had been shoved into the shower stall. All these rooms were equally dusty, cobwebby, and usable, with only the smallest damp stains on the ceilings.

The backyard swarmed with a variety of weeds. While Kay extracted an armful of wood from the clutches of the Johnson grass and blue-flowering mealy sage overgrowing the woodpile behind the bathroom, Liza investigated the windmill. She couldn't figure out how it worked, and the water trough was dry. It looked climbable, but she knew Kay would stop her if she tried.

A barn stood on the edge of the enclosing scrub, the sunset blazing straight through its upper windows. An odd smell came out to meet Liza as she approached, and she hesitated, knowing Kay would tell her not to go in. A door banged. Over her shoulder, Liza saw the back kitchen door swing and no sign of her sister. Liza stepped inside, a single step.

The barn was dark, the sunset light cut off by the

loft above the main room. Gummy somethings squished under her shoes. Above her, something rustled.

"Meow."

Liza turned, but saw only long grass outside, and encroaching scrub. She turned back to the barn. Abandoned skeletons of machinery, whose use she could only guess at, loomed in the dimness. They would be easy to climb.

"Meow."

"*Kschh!*"

Liza leaped back, into the dusk. Already the sunset had faded from the upper window. A vivid white face looked down at her—an inhuman mask. Liza held her breath. A door banged again. The barn owl stretched its wings and sneezed at her.

"What are you doing?" called Kay.

Liza laughed with relief, whirled, and ran toward her. "Did you know barn owls don't hoot?"

"All owls hoot," said Kay scornfully. "Carry in some of those small sticks for kindling, okay?"

"This one doesn't. It sneezes." Liza pulled sticks out of straggling stems of mealy sage while Kay loaded herself with larger wood. "It scared me a minute. And there was a cat out there, too. Can I put out some milk?"

"May as well, since you won't drink evaporated milk. Pick out what you want for supper."

Kay built a fire in the potbellied stove using the dry grass and some brittle newspapers from a box in the next room. Liza got into her sister's pack, opened two cans of ravioli, and dumped them into the saucepan, the smell of tomato paste reminding her how hungry she was. Opening one of the cans of evaporated milk that Kay had bought and Liza had pronounced undrinkable, she poured it into her bowl and put it on the back step. "Kitty, kitty?" Getting no response, she sat watching the sunset gather all its glory into one spot and fade gradually into night. "Kitty, kitty?" An enormous content swelled in her, listening to Kay work, smelling wood smoke, hearing unidentified country rustles, watching the owl float wraithlike from the barn, followed by a rustling, flapping, squeaking cloud—

"Kay! Kay, come look!" Liza stood up, clapping her hands as the bats poured out of the barn—hundreds of them, black and stormy against the dark-blue sky.

"Ugh," said Kay. "There's an awful lot of them!"

"I like bats! My science teacher said if we had more bats we wouldn't need pesticides, because they'd eat up all the mosquitoes."

Kay drew her inside and shut the door. "Leave them alone, okay? They get all tangled in your hair and they carry rabies."

"Mr. Harker says that's an old wives' tale."

"I'd rather believe an old wife than a new science teacher."

They ate ravioli and peanut butter sandwiches by the hot, inadequate light of the stove, splitting the warm remnants of the orange juice they'd bought for breakfast. "I like this place," said Liza. "Wouldn't it be neat if we could live here? You said you wanted to go to a small town."

"I do," said Kay. "It's dumb to run away to a big town where there's drug pushers and things waiting for you. But you can't just show up in a small town and take over any old house, you know. You've got to pay rent, and that means you've got to have a job."

"Maybe the Burgers'll give you a job on their ranch."

"Doing what? I don't know anything about animals."

Liza considered this distasteful reality. "Maybe that man at the station needs a cashier. You can do that."

"Yes." Kay made a slight face. She didn't like working for men. "Even if I can get a job in Britt, we may not be able to rent anything nice."

"I bet the people that own this place'd rent cheap."

"It'd be a long walk to your friends' houses. And you'd have to take the bus to school."

"That's okay." Liza could already see how it would work out. "My friends'll all have bicycles or horses. And I can adopt the cat, and tame armadillos, and learn the organ. It'd be neat!"

Kay laughed but dreamily looked around the soft shadows of the room. "Yeah, it would. And I hate to see a nice little house like this rot to pieces. But it won't happen." She mopped up her tomato sauce with a piece of plain bread.

Liza, recognizing the tone, said nothing.

2

Lies and Luck

Liza woke to an unfamiliar creaking sound, a variety of bird noises, and a dusty mouth. The only sign of Kay was her sleeping bag neatly rolled up and tied. They had slept in the back room, with all the windows open. It was still dim here, but smelled like morning.

Wearing only the underwear she had slept in, Liza went into the backyard through the door in the bedroom's back wall. Standing black against the blue-gray sky, the windmill turned, noisily but steadily. She could see movement through the kitchen window. Something scuttled in the woodpile as she skipped through the damp spiky grass to the kitchen step. The bowl she had left for the cat was gone. "Hey, Kay, the windmill's working!"

Her sister's face appeared in the long window. "I know. As soon as the trough fills up we can—what are you doing with no clothes on? You get in here and get dressed!"

"There's nobody to see me," said Liza, entering. Outside was warm, but the kitchen was hot. Kay's face was already flushed and sweaty. Powdered eggs made unappetizing noises on the stove. "Why're you cooking breakfast? We could have Pop-Tarts."

"We may as well use the stove while we've got it," said Kay.

Liza's bowl sat on the drainboard of the sink, clean and almost dry. "Have you seen the cat?"

"No. And that's another thing. You shouldn't be up running around in the middle of the night."

"I wasn't!" exclaimed Liza indignantly.

"Don't try to tell me stories. The cat certainly didn't get up and wash his own bowl. It was bad enough when you got out of bed at home. It could be dangerous in a place like this."

"I didn't wash any bowl."

"Then how did it get on the drainboard?" Kay waited while Liza looked blankly at the dish. Before she could think of anything to say, Kay continued: "If you're going to tell lies, you'll have to be more careful. Go get dressed."

Liza obeyed, half-angry and half-confused as she dug clean underwear and a T-shirt out of her pack. She hardly ever told lies—certainly not to Kay—and her sister ought to know that. It was true that she often woke up in the middle of the night and was too restless to lie still; but last night, it so happened, she hadn't. So who had washed the bowl? When she sat down to her scrambled eggs (rather dry and singed-looking, with no juice to wash them down), she suggested: "Maybe the cat didn't get the milk. Maybe there was a tramp in the barn."

"The only footprints are ours," said Kay, pointing to the marks in the dust by the sink. "Anyway, what kind of tramp would take a bowl of evaporated milk when he could have robbed us blind?"

"Maybe he didn't want to. Maybe he was a nice tramp."

"You're cruising for a bruising!" snapped Kay. "I don't want to hear any more. It's no big deal you got up last night, but I won't sit here and listen to you lie about it. Okay?"

Liza finished her breakfast in sulky silence. Afterward they took their dirty clothes and the wringer washtub to the trough and did laundry as well as they could. The cold water had a faint brownish cast, and the hand soap would not lather properly. The clothes-line posts were bare of line, so they spread the clothes to dry on the grass and hoped for the best. The day was turning out bright blue and gold, full of intriguing sounds and smells, making Liza feel better in spite of herself.

"We can leave our stuff here while we check the town out," said Kay. "Let me do the talking."

"I can't not answer if somebody talks to me," objected Liza.

"Pretend you're shy."

They were almost to the highway when they heard engine noise. As they moved out of the middle of the road, a dusty Jeep driven by a redneck-looking boy about Kay's age pulled up behind them. The boy regarded them curiously. "Y'all need a lift?"

Liza expected Kay to stick her nose in the air and pretend she hadn't heard, but her sister surprised her. "We're fine," she said, not breaking stride and not quite looking at him.

"You sure?"

"We're on our way to the bus station. It's not far."

"It is if you're walking. Hop in; I'm going there, too."

"No, thank you," said Kay frostily.

"Well—okay." But he waited another whole minute, while Kay kept walking and Liza kept following her, before he put the Jeep in gear again and pulled ahead of them.

"You said never ever to answer a boy who offered you a lift," said Liza when, with one more backward glance, he'd turned onto the highway.

"That's in town," said Kay. "I had to be a little polite to him. We were probably trespassing on his daddy's land."

"Then why not take a lift?"

"Never risk your life just to be polite."

"Oh." Probably Kay knew best; but it was a long walk.

The Jeep and a couple of dirty pickups were parked outside the bus station. A nondescript dog got up from behind the Coke machine and barked at them. "Oh, hush up, Fred," said a voice from inside, and the man who had been at the cash register last night came to the door. "Don't pay him any mind, ladies. He likes me to think he's on the job, but I know better. I'm Phil Guerra. What can I do for you?"

"I don't hardly know," said Kay with unaccustomed politeness as he stood aside for them to go in. The station was dark and stuffy after the morning brightness. Liza had to blink three times before she could see anything. "We came here on a forlorn hope, and it doesn't look like it's working out. What happened to the people that used to live on the old Stark place?"

"Good night!" exclaimed a dried-up man, of uncertain age, drinking a cup of coffee with his cap on at the counter. "Honey, ain't nobody lived there since old Aunt Enid died, six, seven years back."

The boy from the Jeep also sat at the counter, the large cardboard box that had been unloaded last night and a Dr Pepper in front of him. "So that's where y'all had been," he said. "You should've come with me. I could've told you all about it."

"Aunt Enid?" said Kay to the dried-up man. "Were you related to the Starks?"

He shook his head. "Everybody called her Aunt Enid. What you want with the Stark place, anyhow?"

"Well—it's only a hunch. See, our grandma's—our mom's mom's—maiden name was Stark, or Stack, or something like that." Liza avoided looking in the men's faces as Kay told this fib. She didn't know what Grandma's birth name was, but it probably wasn't Stark. "And I kind of thought the name of the town she was from was Britt. I'd forgotten about it till we saw the city limits sign. So I thought we'd check it out, and we found the Stark place, all right. But there wasn't anybody there."

"You were on the bus last night, weren't you?" asked Mr. Guerra. "You should've told somebody you were going. The driver noticed he was short two girls, and they held up half an hour looking for you."

"Oh, I'm sorry about that!" Kay sounded genuinely upset—not surprisingly, after all her care to go unnoticed. "I was so excited about maybe finding some family I didn't think about anything. And then when we found the place deserted, we decided we might as well camp out."

The dried-up man whistled. "You girls camped out in the haunted homestead? I wouldn't do that for a hundred dollars!"

"Haunted?" gasped Liza.

"Shut up, Clovis," said the boy. "You don't need to go around scaring little girls."

Mr. Guerra eyed Kay thoughtfully. "Y'all out looking for your roots?"

"Uh—not exactly." Liza wondered if Kay's nervousness were real or faked, then recalled the way she had looked at their stepfather, Lee, as she patted the baseball bat, and dismissed the notion that Kay was ever nervous. "We're one step ahead of the social workers, really. See, our folks . . . um . . . died"—three faces winced in sympathy—"in a car accident right before school let out, and we'd pretty much lost track of the rest of the family. We used to move around a lot, you know. Anyhow, I'm plenty old enough to look after Liza, but the lady from the county didn't seem to think so, and we figured it'd be easier just to light out."

"Good for you," said Clovis.

"I'm sorry about your mom and dad," said the boy. "That's real rough on you."

"It is," agreed the cashier. "And your grandma was one of the Stark girls? Do you know which one?"

Kay shrugged. "It might not even be this Stark. I'm vaguely remembering something Mom said when I wasn't listening."

"Willa taught school in Amarillo for a while," said Clovis thoughtfully, "and I thought I heard Mavis was dead or sick or something. But I ain't seen one of them since they came up for the funeral and had that big fight over who owned what. What about it, Stu? Your granddad ever hear from them?"

"Granddad doesn't hear from anybody but the mail-order companies and the sweepstakes," said the boy.

Kay sighed. "Oh, well. We were thinking how nice it'd be to find some relatives here and get a job and maybe rent that nice little house cheap from our long-lost uncle, or something. I guess it belongs to those Burgers on the other mailbox now, though."

"Nope," said Stu. "It doesn't belong to anybody."

"Everything belongs to somebody," said Liza. She was tired of standing around, so she climbed on a stool, three removed from Clovis, and spun herself. The vinyl was slick under her jeans.

"Not necessarily," said Mr. Guerra. "You get out here in these little towns, where oil's gone bust and all the jobs dried up, you can find lots of houses it'd take a long hunt to find the owners for. It's not even worth the government's while to take them over. That's the only reason we can keep up our own school—we've got houses we can let the teachers have rent free, and that keeps the salaries down."

Kay's eyes lit up. "So if Liza and I wanted to move in and stay while I looked for a job, nobody'd stop us?"

"It'd be nobody's business to," said Mr. Guerra. "Heck, it probably belongs to you as much as anybody."

Clovis pulled a can of snuff out of his back pocket and carefully stuffed his lip. "Don't go getting your hopes up, little lady. There ain't no open jobs in Britt."

"Hold on a minute," said Mr. Guerra, before Kay had time to look disappointed. "That worthless Phelps boy didn't show up this morning again, and I told him a week ago I wasn't putting up with that no more. So there's one job needs filling. You ever work a cash register?"

"Oh, yeah!" said Kay eagerly. "I've worked at McDonald's, and Wendy's, and the front desk in the beauty parlor Mom worked at. Only—if I give you references, the social worker might track us down."

"Don't worry about that. I owe Aunt Enid some favors I never could pay back while she was alive. Besides, you can't be any worse at the job than Randy Phelps."

This place was more of an icehouse, or general store, than a bus or gas station, with shelves of canned goods, fishing tackle, and ice chests. Liza poked among the comic books and magazines while Kay talked about hours and pay and boring stuff like that. All the comic books were at least three months old. After a while, Clovis said something about an old lady waiting for him and left. Liza followed him. "Sir? How's the Stark place haunted?"

"What d'you mean, how?" He spat in the gravel. "It's haunted. Always was, far back as I remember."

"So it's not Aunt Enid's ghost?"

"Land, no. She was real good friends with the haunt. Said he was a real help around the house, but us Yanks—and that's what she called us—didn't understand that kind of thing. And then she'd always get in a fight for calling us Yanks. She was a Limey, you know—English—married Rankin Stark during the war."

Liza wanted to ask which war but didn't think it would fit with being related, so she nodded. "How does a ghost help around the house? Did it wash dishes or something?"

"I don't know. That's what she said. It used to embarrass her kids something awful. Even after they were most grown, if they as much as left their socks under the bed, Aunt Enid'd threaten 'em with the haunt. 'Hobkin'll get tha for that,' she'd say. Always said 'tha' for 'you,' I don't know why."

"It's an awful clean house still," said Liza, "except for the dust. The windmill works and everything."

"Does it? Ain't that something! It must be wasting water all over the yard!"

"Well, it wasn't working last night, but it was this morning when we woke up."

Clovis nodded and spat. "That'll be the haunt. It must've recognized you. Mostly kids that try to come around at night leave again in a mighty big hurry, but I guess if you're Aunt Enid's great-grandkids, it'll figure you've got a right to be there."

Thinking of all the lies Kay had told that morning, Liza felt uneasy. "What—what happens to the kids that have to leave quick?"

"Better ask Stu about that. He's your near neighbor, you know. The Burger place is about five miles up the road there, past the creek." He spat again, and cleared his throat. "I got to get going, little lady. See you around."

He drove off, leaving Liza with plenty to think about.

3

Keeping House

_____ *Kay started working at the store at* once, leaving Liza to do grown-up things like clean the house and meet the man who came out to hook up the utilities. Utility, as it turned out; the house's wiring had gone bad, and the clay pipes leading from the well to the house had collapsed, so all they had in the house was gas, though the windmill faithfully kept the trough full of warm, strong-tasting water. The metal-lined cabinet turned out to be an old-fashioned icebox, so Kay brought home bags of ice every couple of days, and they kept their eggs and milk cool there. Liza felt adventurous and pioneery, using the smelly, dark outhouse behind the barn, contriving furniture out of crates Mr. Guerra let them have, and running in and out for water.

Every night Liza put out milk for the invisible cat, and every morning found the dish clean and drying on the drainboard. After Kay brought home a bag of coffee and an old-fashioned tin coffee pot, morning coffee also began to appear, brewing on the back of the stove. Liza took care to get up first in the morning so she would find these things instead of Kay. She didn't want Kay scolding her for running around at night again. Besides, it was her mystery, not Kay's. Kay wanted no part of it. Rising at the first paling of darkness was easy, because without electricity, she had to go to bed as soon as the daylight failed in the evening.

Kay thought it was as silly to feed a cat they never saw as to believe in haunting. "You're just pouring money away, giving it milk," she complained.

"But someday it might get tame," Liza pointed out. "You have to be patient with animals. Anyway, we can't drink the milk fast enough, and it's better the cat should get it before it spoils." Kay had to concede that. The icebox didn't keep things cold well, compared to a refrigerator.

One morning Liza got up in time to see a family of skunks disappear under the bathroom. She had cold cereal for breakfast, saw Kay off to work, and got bored immediately. The floor was dusty again, but she had already swept four times that week. The idea of washing clothes made her back ache. She had no TV or radio, no books except her word-find puzzles, and she had worked all of those. If she made the long, hot walk to town, there would be nothing to do once she got there. Half the stores were empty, and all the girls her age, according to Mr. Guerra, had gone to Girl Scout camp. What sort of town was it, Liza wondered crossly, in which all the girls were Scouts?

She went into the parlor and tried to get the organ to work, but all she raised was dust. Apart from the floor having been swept, and all the windows having been opened for the cross breeze, this room was just as she and Kay had found it. They really had no use for it, except as a place to pile up aluminum for recycling. Giving up on the organ, Liza started digging through the box of newspapers. Though yellow and crumbling, they were not old enough to be interesting—not even as old as she was. Clouds of dust rose as she handled the brittle pages, startling a sneeze out of her and making her eyes itch. Ugh! She'd better throw them away down the outhouse, Liza decided. Now that they had gas, they didn't need the paper to light the wood stove. She began taking them out an armload at a time.

On the third trip she emptied the box down to some fragments of broken newsprint, a dead cricket, and three brown spiral notebooks. Liza dropped the paper and opened a notebook. Faded black handwriting covered the yellowed paper in short, unindented paragraphs separated by dates. The first entry was for 4 Aug 21.

Liza's heart thumped in her chest. Old diaries! She had read about old diaries! They were always fascinating and often gave Nancy Drew or whoever clues. What had happened 4 Aug 21? The handwriting made her feel cross-eyed, but she puzzled it out. "Fine baby boy 7 lbs 12 oz. 2 AM. Rankin Jr. Dr. late, Hobkin very helpful."

Abandoning the last armload of paper, Liza got a Coke out of the icebox and sat on a crate on the gallery to read. The windmill creaked, locusts buzzed, and a horny toad (Kay said horned toad; but everyone around here called them horny toads, and Liza figured they should know) scurried between two cedar poles to disappear in the long, dry grass. Deciphering the handwriting in the diaries made her head ache, and the result was often not worth the effort.

"Ranny 8 lbs 3 oz. Cotton too small."

"This heat will kill me. Rankin laughs, says this is normal. Never would have finished wash without Hobkin."

"Ranny 9 lbs. Killed scorpion by woodpile."

Some entries were only lists of household chores or of prices for eggs, milk, and butter that seemed surprisingly low to Liza. She wished things were that cheap now. Kay wouldn't complain about money so much. She didn't see why they had to worry about money, anyway. After emptying Kay's college fund and selling both their bikes and Kay saving her allowance for who knew how long, they had had a couple of thousand dollars to put in the scruffy little bank in Britt. The woman writing this diary had real money problems—two whole pages were devoted to writing down what they needed to buy, adding it up, crossing things out, and adding again, until she got the whole winter clothes budget for herself, Rankin, and the baby down to twelve dollars. Hobkin didn't get any clothes. Liza wondered who Hobkin was and who was writing the diary. It might be Aunt Enid, but it might not be.

Liza picked up another notebook and flipped through it. More of the same. Nita was born 16 Sep 24, and someone named Mavis had come along in between. On 5 Nov 24 the diarist got homesick and held her own Guy Fawkes celebration, whatever that was, with a bonfire in the yard and a scarecrow. Rankin laughed at her, but the children enjoyed it. Hobkin kept Ranny from scalding himself in the wash water.

Chore lists, prices. Liza yawned. Unhopefully, she picked up the third notebook and a picture fell out. It showed the house; a woman with short hair and a dress like a sack, holding a baby; two little girls and a little boy; a thin, dried-out man; and a Model T. Yellow spots of dried glue on the notebook's inside front cover showed where the picture had been attached, with familiar handwriting underneath that identified the people as Enid (me), Rankin, Ranny, Nita, Mavis, and Baby Larry.

Having at last confirmed that the diaries belonged to Aunt Enid, Liza lost all interest and put them away in the crate she used as a shelf in the back bedroom, next to her word-find book and her hairbrush. She might as well have lunch now. There was nothing else to do. She ate peanut butter and jelly, drank some milk, and rinsed her dishes at the tub by the trough. The sky was white with heat.

Liza went to the door of the barn, dark and cool and smelly—that same odd smell. It must be the bats. Kay had told her not to go in because of the bats and because the farm machinery was dangerous to play on. Kay was such a worrywart. Liza wasn't afraid of bats. Still, the thought of walking on that bat mess all over the floor, even in tennis shoes, was pretty icky. If she were back home, she could go over to Mary Alice's and they'd hang out watching game shows or playing clapping games till they'd digested lunch enough to go swimming. A lump gathered in Liza's throat. She missed Mary Alice. She missed Mom. She even— though she'd as soon cut her tongue out as tell Kay— missed Lee. Ignoring the memory of the times she had heard Mom crying in the night and the day Lee flushed her own goldfish down the toilet, Liza thought about all the good things she had left behind. Her eyes began to sting.

"Meow."

Liza turned. "Meow." The cat had to be in the Johnson grass on the edge of the mesquite. "Kitty, kitty?" she called, wading cautiously into the scrub. With mesquite, cactus, and burrs, there was plenty to be cautious of in this yard. Liza became a hunter on safari, tracking the rare miniature tiger—not to kill it, of course. To live with it and study it, like that lady on TV that time, who lived with the gorillas. She hadn't been able to see the end of that movie. Lee had switched to some boring sports show in the middle.

She was about ready to give up on a safari with so many thorns, and with such elusive prey, when she found a path. It was too small to get a truck through, about wide enough for a skinny cow. Leaving the cat to its own devices, Liza followed the track, remembering after a few feet to pick up a stick in case she met a rattler. She soon found that the stick was also useful to push branches and baby mesquites aside. Since the ground under the scrub was mostly bare of grass, it was hard to tell where the path went at first; but she soon came out onto open terrain.

The mesquite thicket made the Stark place unusually private. Now, outside it, she could see at least a hundred miles. Though the population sign was well out on the highway, the town didn't begin till you got to the co-op, and then it was still a ways to downtown. Those low buildings way over there, with the windmill, would be the Burger ranch; and off to the left were the water tower and the huddled buildings of Britt. She could even see the Burgers' cattle, red dots in the distance. The only variety to a landscape of creosote, mesquite, and cactus was a dark line of cedars. Liza walked toward these.

The cedars were farther away than they looked, and Liza had to crawl through a barbed wire fence to get there. Soon her mouth was sticky with thirst and her head aching. She should not have come away without her canteen and hat! And what if she got lost among all these cattle trails? By the time these prudent thoughts occurred to her, however, it made as much sense to go on as to go back. She hurried to get into the shade— and almost fell down the creek bank.

Liza grabbed sticky, flat cedar leaves to steady herself. They broke off in her hands, but she had her balance back. "Oh, wow," she said. "It's practically a canyon!" A little brown water ran over white dirt at the bottom. The sides were steep but craggy with outthrust roots and rocks. She got down with only a little scraping on her hands and arms, sat on a rock, and took off her shoes and socks. The water was a muddy color, and slimy moss broke the surface in places; but she was too thirsty to care, and figured it couldn't be too awfully polluted out here. It tasted bad. Liza rolled up her jeans and stuck her feet in. That was better. The water wasn't cool, but it wasn't as hot as the air, either. Hanging her shoes, with the socks stuffed inside, round her neck by the laces, she waded upstream.

The creek got deeper and the bank lower as she went. Shoals of tiny fish darted out of her way. She had to watch her feet constantly, since some parts of the bed were soft mud or moss, and others sharp rock. She was considering walking on the dry part of the channel bottom instead—there was room, mostly— and wondering how to dry her feet before putting her socks back on, when she heard splashing, shouting in English and Spanish, and the sound of a mad animal bawling ahead.

Liza pricked up her ears. That could be almost anything—a dangerous criminal, or cowboys, or—anything! She sneaked along under the bank, her braids and her shoes dangling inconveniently over her shoulders. When she could see what was going on, she crouched down.

A boy was wrestling with a black goat, trying to drag it out of the creek by means of a rope leash. The goat put up a glorious resistance, straining backward, skipping sideways, and bleating as if it were being murdered. Amid the flying water, one face was about as stubborn as the other. Liza was making up her mind which one to root for, when the goat jerked the rope free of the boy's hands. The boy lunged to recover it, and fell facedown in brown water while the goat danced out the other side.

4

Enid the Goat

Liza laughed and splashed to the boy's aid, but he had already picked himself up, throwing dirty looks indiscriminately at her and at the goat, who stood on the bank opposite him rolling its yellow eyes and bleating as if it were laughing, too. "Are you okay?" Liza asked.

"Oh, I'm fine," said the boy. "It's La Bruja there that's dogmeat."

"Baaaa." The goat's bleat was louder.

"I'll help you catch her," offered Liza.

"I don't need help from a city girl that don't know any better than to wade barefoot in a creek full of water mocassins," said the boy, slinging black, wet hair out of his eyes.

"I haven't seen any mocassins," said Liza, but she

climbed onto the bank. "How do you know I'm a city girl?"

"I'm not dumb, that's how. You got to be that girl that moved into the Stark place, and Stu says y'all are from San Antonio. Anyhow, only a city girl'd be out here without boots. You're asking to get bit by a rattler."

"I'm not dumb, either," retorted Liza. "If I hear a rattle, I'll stand dead still till it goes away."

"You might not hear a rattle." The boy sat beside her, wringing out his shirttail and adopting a confidential, story-telling tone. "Mr. Burger found him a seven-foot-long rattler up by the house a while back. So he killed it; but it was getting on for dark, and he had to finish his chores, and by the time he came back to skin it, there wasn't enough light. But Miz Burger wouldn't let him bring it up on the porch."

"I don't blame her," said Liza.

"He knew the dogs'd spoil it if he left it in the yard all night. So he figured he'd at least get the rattle. You know those snakes add a rattle every time they shed a skin, so by the time one's old enough to be seven foot long, it's pretty big." He stopped wringing his shirt and began acting out the story with his hands. "So Mr. Burger gets a flashlight and his bowie knife, and goes out in the yard, and feels around till he gets hold of that rattle, and chops it off. It's about yea big"— holding his hands six inches apart—"and he figures he can put it on a pin to decorate his hat. But he goes out in the yard in the morning and, sure enough, the dogs've been at the snake, and the skin's all ruined. But the rattles are still on."

From the way he said it, this was obviously supposed to be highly significant. "So he only got half the rattle?"

"No, dummy! There'd been another snake out there that was just as big, and he'd chopped its rattle off! And it was alive!"

Apparently her reaction was satisfactory this time. He smiled triumphantly. "So now there's a seven-foot rattler out here somewhere that can't warn you it's coming!"

Liza bent over to roll down her jeans, while casting a nervous glance around. "Your goat's getting away," she said, glad at the chance to undercut him so quickly.

The goat strolled up the creek, gnawing on cedar and rubbing her horns against eroded roots. The boy scowled at her. "I don't care! She's nothing but trouble! Are you Kay or Liza?"

"Liza. Who are you?"

"Vic Guerra. My dad works for Mr. Burger."

"Are you related to Phil Guerra that owns the store?"

"He's my uncle," said Vic, with a touch of pride. "He lets me pick out what comic books to order."

Liza gave up trying to dry her feet and put on her socks. "Then you should tell him to get them sooner," she said. "I read all the comics in that store ages ago."

"Oh, you liar! Those are all this month's comics."

"Yeah, but a real comic store like we have at home

gets them at least a month before the date on the cover, usually more." Having scored a point, she changed the subject quickly. "You worked awful hard trying to get that goat. You going to let it beat you now?"

Vic grimaced. "Oh, I'm sick to death of chasing her! This is the third time this week she got loose." He shook his fist at the beast, who scrambled a little farther up the bank, the rope trailing between her legs in a manner that looked dangerous to Liza. "And she's no good for anything. I didn't get any ribbons with her at the rodeo, and nobody offered me a good price for her, and her wool's only ordinary. I got half a mind to barbecue her at the Fourth of July picnic."

Liza gasped. "But that's awful! Isn't she a pet?"

"Pets are for city folks," said Vic scornfully. "Out here you got to be practical."

"But doesn't she give milk or something?"

"We got lots of goats to milk if we want it. And it's just one more chore for me. She's not worth the aggravation. But I guess I ought to go get her."

Vic crossed the creek in two steps, using a flat rock in the middle as a stepping stone. Liza, thinking hard, followed him. "How much are goats worth?" she asked.

"Oh, depends. Sometimes you can get a couple hundred a head," said Vic, creeping up on the browsing goat. Just as he was about to lay hands on the rope, she skipped aside and bounded up the bank with a mocking bleat. Vic said a bad word in Spanish.

All Liza had of her own was a five-dollar bill and

some change—the remains of a ten Kay had given her when they first ran away. "But if you're going to kill her for barbecue, she can't be worth anything like that much," she said, scrambling after him.

"She's not worth two cents," said Vic disgustedly. She was eating again, munching away at a clump of bear grass. "Look, if you're going to tag along, at least try and be useful. Go around there and see if you can chase her toward me."

Liza did her best, but the goat ran in the wrong direction and she was unable to catch the rope as the goat went by. As they gave chase, she called to Vic: "I'll give you a dollar for her!"

"Get stuffed! She's worth more than that as barbecue!"

It took them a half hour to get hold of her again, and then it was only because she got tired of playing and became suddenly tame. By that time Vic was ready to part with her for five dollars, collar and feed thrown in free. "But you'll be sorry," he warned.

"What did you call her before?" asked Liza, as they led the goat back toward the mesquite around the Stark place.

"La Bruja," said Vic. "I call her that because all goats have the devil in them."

"That's a terrible name," objected Liza. She knew all about brujas. They gave people the evil eye, and a few years ago the Mexican police had arrested a ranch full of brujas that were kidnapping people to eat. "No wonder she won't behave, with a name like that."

35

"She'd act the same no matter what name I gave her."

"Names are very important." Liza felt like an authority on the matter. "If my name were different—like if it were Sara, or something—I'd be a whole different person. Saras are all gentle and dreamy."

"Oh, garbage. You can call her Sara if you want, but she'll still be an ornery old goat."

"I'll call her Enid, after my great-grandmother." There. She'd told outright the lie she'd been living all week. It made her feel settled, somehow; as if everything up to now had been reversible. She tugged the newly christened Enid away from a Spanish dagger plant she'd stopped to sniff.

"It's a stupid name," said Vic.

They argued the matter all the way to the mesquite path, when Vic struck a more interesting topic. "You seen the ghost yet?" he asked, pushing Enid while Liza pulled.

"No," said Liza, "but it's here. Every night I put out a bowl of milk for this cat that hangs around, and every morning when I get up the bowl's been washed already, plus the coffee's started. And the ghost started the windmill for us. The man that came to look at the water and gas and stuff said he was sure the pump had been disconnected when Aunt Enid died, but it connected itself up and started pumping water the first night we were here. And that's impossible!"

They tied Enid to the clothesline post with the rope and an extra length of clothesline. Liza got her money out of the side pocket of her backpack, paid Vic, and showed him around. He didn't mind going into the bat-messy barn and wanted to see the owl nest, but there was no ladder to the loft and they couldn't figure out another way to get up. After that they were filthy, so they washed their hands and faces by the trough and sat on the back step with a bag of Oreos between them, watching Enid eagerly cropping weeds.

"I met the ghost once," said Vic. "Last Halloween. Me and Jerry Post got dared to come up here at midnight, so I snuck out and borrowed Stu's horse. So I got here, and that chicken Jerry never showed up. But I figured I better go through with it and prove I'd been here; so I tried to lead the horse up the pickup track, but he wouldn't come. So I tied him to a tree branch and came on foot. And I got lost."

"How do you get lost on that little, short path?" asked Liza scornfully.

"Everything was different. I walked, and I walked, and I never came out of the trees. I saw a light, like a flashlight; but when I called—I thought maybe it was Jerry, so I called out—nobody answered. I kept walking and walking and not getting anywhere."

"What'd you do?"

"Finally I remembered to make the sign of the cross." He demonstrated, crossing himself from forehead to chest and from shoulder to shoulder. "You should always make the sign of the cross if there's ghosts around. And suddenly I was right in front of the house, and the light was gone. So I took the chalk

I'd brought and went up to the door to write my name on it. Suddenly the door flew open, and something grabbed me and started pinching me all over!"

"Oooh! What'd it look like?"

"That was the worst part! I was being beat on and pinched and shook, and there wasn't anything there!" He paused to enjoy her reaction. "So I dropped the chalk, and I ran! All the way back to the horse, with the branches hitting me in the face, and I jumped on like one of those cowboys in the corny old westerns, and we lit out of there!"

"I thought you'd tied the horse," objected Liza.

"I did! I'd forgot all about it; and when the horse jerked to a stop, I thought the ghost had us! Then I saw where I'd tied the reins, and this white thing swooped down at me out of the sky; so I pulled out my knife and cut right through them! And that old horse moved faster than it ever had before!"

"That white thing was probably the owl," Liza pointed out.

"That's what Stu said. I had to tell him what happened, because of spoiling his bridle and sweating his horse up. But I had the bruises all over me, and nobody could say how I got lost without leaving the track."

Liza wondered why, if the ghost resented intruders so much, it had been nice to her and Kay. Maybe they had accidentally told the truth and they really were related to the Starks someway. "Do you know who it's the ghost of?"

"Oh, that's easy. It's got to be Aunt Enid's kid Larry that got snakebit. You can see his headstone over in the graveyard. He died from a rattlesnake bite right here in the backyard, and ever since that time there's never been a rattlesnake around this house because Larry keeps them out."

Larry. Liza thought of the baby in the picture, intending to feel sad for him, but Vic kept talking, leaving her no time. He knew lots of stories, about teenagers who had been run off when they tried to come here to park on dates, and mysterious lights, and so on. Not to be outdone, Liza told him about the railroad crossing in San Antonio where the ghosts of kids that had died when their bus stalled would push stopped cars off the track. Then he told her about the Goat Man, which meant she had to tell him about the Donkey Lady; and they were still trying to top each other when Kay got home.

Vic stood up when he saw her, dropping crumbs off his lap. "Isn't it kind of late for you to be out?" she asked pointedly.

"Oh, I was just going," he said.

"Don't forget your goat," said Kay, seeing him walk right past Enid.

"Oh, that's hers now," said Vic. "Fair and square. Bye."

Liza felt small when Kay looked at her. "You bought a goat?"

"It was only five dollars," said Liza defensively. "It'll pay for itself in two weeks, 'cause we won't have to buy milk anymore. And you've been worrying about how long the grass is—she'll keep it cut short."

"And who do you expect to milk this living lawn-mower?"

"I will. I've seen it on TV lots of times."

"Oh, for crying out loud!" Kay sounded tired and disgusted. "You're filthy, and you brought a strange boy into our house, and I bet you've spoiled your appetite with all those cookies! What am I going to do with you?"

Liza brushed herself off, noticing that, between one thing and another, her T-shirt was almost black and her jeans weren't much better. She was glad the worst of her muddy socks were covered by her muddy shoes. "Well, nobody told you to bring me," she said crossly. "You could've run away all by yourself."

Kay's expression changed, becoming soft and shaky. "No. No, I couldn't. But there's no point fighting. Go ahead and take your bath now, and maybe then you'll have an appetite."

The evening was pretty awful. Liza had to force herself to eat the dinner Kay made—a local dish called Frito pie, consisting of chili poured over corn chips—but she had eaten too many Oreos to enjoy it. Kay found the last of the newspapers from the box torn and scattered all over the parlor, and Liza had to finish throwing them out and suffer a scolding about making a mess, as well. She couldn't figure how they'd gotten into such a state. All the pages had been separated out and then torn to bits, a feat that should have been beyond any high wind or animal.

Then it came time to milk Enid. It looked simple when farm women did it on TV—but they had pails, and low stools, and, most importantly, large, placid cows to work with. Liza had the saucepan, still damp from washing out the chili, and had to kneel; and Enid would not stand still. They tried everything—tying her head and tail both to the clothespost, having Liza soothe her with a handful of grass while Kay tried to milk, even singing lullabies. Enid pranced, kicked, snapped, bleated, and rolled her flat yellow eyes wickedly till the light was gone, Kay was screaming, and Liza was crying with frustration.

"Never mind," said Kay, getting control of herself and giving Liza a hug. "We'll leave her tied up like that, and maybe she'll be more reasonable in the morning. Let that teach you not to be conned by strange boys."

"It's not Vic's fault," sniffed Liza, following her into the house. "He told me she was worthless. But I thought it was such a neat idea to have a goat, and save money on milk, and everything. I'm sorry."

"Don't worry about it. You'll know better next time."

Liza brushed her teeth under the reproachful gaze of the uncomfortably bound Enid and went to bed. She was just settling in, feeling heavy all over, when Kay sat down on the foot of her sleeping bag, a gray mound in the moonlight. "Liza? I need you to promise me something."

"What?"

"Don't let Vic come here when I'm not around."

"Why not? He's okay. He's Mr. Guerra's nephew. And he's the only kid my age in town, practically."

"I don't care if he's Prince Charles's nephew. I don't want you being all alone with him, or any other boy— or man, either, unless it's the gas man or somebody."

Liza tried to think about this. Kay had always been warning her about strange men in San Antonio, but things must be different in Britt. "But—if there were any bad kind of people around here, everybody'd know who they were, and they'd warn us."

"You can't ever be sure about men," said Kay decidedly. "They can seem as nice as can be, and as soon as they think they can get away with it, pow!"

Liza wondered what Kay meant by "pow!" exactly, but she didn't like to ask. She was sleepy and knew Kay wouldn't go away till she'd gotten what she wanted. "Okay," she yawned. "I promise."

"Good girl." Kay kissed her.

Liza woke suddenly. Chunks of moonlight lay on the floor. Nearby the windmill creaked. Far away something howled. She had heard those howls before, assuming them to be dogs; but Vic had said they were coyotes. Did coyotes eat goats? Serve Enid right if they did; but she didn't like the idea of finding a mangled goat carcass in the morning.

Suddenly it occurred to her that she had not set out the cat's milk. Shoving her feet into her shoes, she went via the yard so as not to disturb Kay, got the milk out of the icebox, and set it on the back step. Enid bleated, stamping her feet and staring at Liza out of a tangle of rope.

"Poor Enid. We didn't leave you enough slack to lie down." With a good deal of fumbling, Liza untied the clothesline around Enid's tail and petted her soft, matted back. She wondered if you were supposed to brush goats. Enid made an unexpectedly gentle noise and lay down. Liza went back to bed.

5

Mrs. Burger's Box

_____ *Liza woke while the backyard was* still in shadow and lay drowsily listening to the bats returning home through the coffee-scented morning. Kay had given her orders to wash her jeans today. She would have to haul water in from the trough, heat it on the stove, and then haul it, bit by bit, outside again before she could even start the washing part. She knew because she had to do this almost every day now. When they ran away, they had stuffed their packs till they almost couldn't close, but they still had hardly any clothes. Kay had promised they could go shopping on Monday, but Liza was not hopeful. Britt didn't even have a mall.

Eventually she dressed and went outside. Enid nibbled a thistle as peacefully as if she had never kicked over a saucepan in her life. "You going to let us milk you today?" asked Liza.

Enid chewed, the horizontal pupils in her eyes making her look as if she were plotting something unspeakably wicked. Mr. Harker said that there were no wicked animals, because they had no concept of right and wrong—only of what they could and couldn't get away with. Hesitantly, Liza scratched Enid behind the horns. She seemed to like it.

Now seemed as good a time as any to try milking her again. Liza went into the kitchen. The bowl she had set out last night was on the drainboard as usual, but she couldn't find the saucepan. It wasn't on its hook over the gas stove, or on top of either stove, or on top of the icebox or the crate they used as a pantry, and that was about all the places it could be. Liza gave up and got herself a bowl of puffed wheat. When she opened the icebox, the saucepan, with its lid on, was next to the milk carton. "What the—?" Liza uncovered the pan. It was three-quarters full of slightly warm milk. She looked around, suddenly chilly in the warm morning. A horny toad sat on the windowsill, its throat pulsing gently.

Kay was drinking coffee and Liza was eating cereal, with goat's milk, on the gallery, when Enid began to bawl and an engine approached down the truck track. The sisters looked at each other, tensing. Why would anybody come here at this hour?

The Burgers' Jeep bounced slowly into the yard,

and Mrs. Burger waved cheerily. Liza relaxed. Mrs. Burger had come by once before to say hello. She was a dumpy woman with tulip-shaped glasses and gray hair that needed to go back to the beauty parlor—harmless, if a little loud. "Good morning!" she called, stopping her engine. "I hear y'all went into the live-stock business!"

"Yes, ma'am," said Kay. "And Liza's already figured out how to milk! She got up at the crack of dawn and got us a panful."

Kay sounded so proud of what she assumed her sister had done that Liza wanted to crawl down a hole. Mrs. Burger didn't make things any better. "Good for you! She give you any trouble?"

"She did last night," said Liza, "but she was okay this morning." Which was true, as far as it went.

"I expect she was pretty uncomfortable by that time," said Mrs. Burger, getting out and pulling a box with a pie plate balanced on top out of the passenger seat. "When Vic told us about it, I figured I'd run over with a few things he should've included in the purchase price, and then I turned up some stuff we weren't using anyway, and I'd just finished baking more pies than we needed to eat, so now I'm a little loaded down. No, no, I'll manage. Y'all finish your breakfast. I can give you a lift to the store if you want, Kay. I got to run into town for a part for the washer, anyway. Wouldn't you know it'd be the washer that breaks down? I could last till November without a drying machine, but I won't last a day without washing a load."

Mrs. Burger barely shut up the whole time she was there. Liza heard more about goats than she could expect to remember. Mrs. Burger had brought a covered metal pail, which she warned Liza to keep absolutely clean and never, ever use for anything else but milking; and bottles of disinfectant, a frightening assortment of grooming implements, the feed Vic had promised her, and other supplies, as well as a box of books and a buttermilk pie. When Kay tried to get stiff and proud about accepting it all, Mrs. Burger brushed her protests aside—keeping a goat without all this stuff was impossible, the books were old ones they never read anyway, and the pie was just neighborly. She showed Liza how to wash Enid's udder, and inadvertently showed her how to milk by checking to make sure she'd gotten all the milk that morning. Liza was so embarrassed at being praised for her thoroughness in a job she hadn't performed that she hardly caught a word.

"It's not a good idea to keep her tethered," said Mrs. Burger. "We'll take you out to the dump sometime and get you some old bedsprings for a fence. Meantime she'll be better off tied to a mesquite. Better forage. They don't like grass, you know. Just weeds and bushes and my roses. I brought you another bucket to water her with. You've been letting her drink out of your trough? Well, it's your drinking water!" It was a relief when Mrs. Burger and Kay rode off in the Jeep, leaving Liza and Enid to themselves.

Well, not quite to themselves. Wondering guiltily

whether keeping rattlesnakes off the property was hard work and if it was hard for a ghost to milk a goat, Liza made herself start water heating for washing and brushed out Enid's coat before she looked in the box of books. It contained a manual on goat care, a cookbook, a Girl Scout Handbook, and some pamphlets from the 4H Club; a couple of Harlequin romances and Nancy Drew mysteries; *Old Yeller*; several horse stories; and, at the very bottom, something called *An Encyclopedia of Fairies*. All were in paperback, except the Nancy Drews; and everything but the fairy book showed signs of either poor care or constant use, with torn or missing covers, dog ears, and even notes written in the margins on the handbooks. Liza had never cared much about fairies, but the book about them was so different from the others that she opened it first, out of curiosity. "Happy Birthday Sara from Aunt Enid," read the familiar handwriting on the title page.

Liza slammed the book shut, her heart thumping. Nobody here could know—nobody—and, anyway, Aunt Enid was dead! That last thought was not as helpful as it would have been a week ago.

She put the books away in the crate next to the puzzles and the diaries and lit into housework to keep from thinking. The house always needed sweeping, the stove top was dirty, and they had never cleaned the ashes out of the wood stove after the gas was turned on. The laundry was a perfectly enormous job all by itself, especially since the water was so hard the soap refused to make anything but the smallest, most depressed-looking suds. Enid kept chewing on her tether, or straining to come see what Liza was doing, or distracting her by dancing in place and tangling her legs in the rope. When Liza was too worn out to work anymore, she found some shade and read about goat care while drinking Coke and keeping an eye on Enid. This did not really make her feel rested. If she had known how much work a goat would be, she never would have offered Vic fifty cents! Still, it would be too embarrassing to back out now.

Kay also looked exhausted when she got home, shoulders bent with her burden of ice from the station and groceries from the co-op. This time she also brought a couple of buckets she had bought.

"I wish you'd thought of those earlier," complained Liza. "I had to run back and forth with the saucepan all day today."

"Well, I'm sorry if I inconvenienced you," retorted Kay, opening a can of roast beef hash. "Miz Burger wants us to come for Sunday dinner tomorrow."

"Good. I'm sick of all this canned stuff."

"If you don't like it, cook for yourself!" Kay angrily scraped the hash into the frying pan. "I'm standing up all day selling snuff to rednecks and listening to little old ladies tell me about Aunt Enid and being Mr. Guerra's perfect employee. I don't have the energy to come home and cook chicken dinners!"

"Mom used to work all day and then cook."

"If I were as dumb as Mom we wouldn't be here."

"Yeah, we'd be in San Antonio, where there's malls and electricity and running water and air-conditioning and movies and people to play with!" Liza had not started out to shout, but by the time she reached the end of the sentence, she was. "What's so smart about you?"

Kay set the frying pan on the blue flame of the stove, walked over to Liza, took her by the shoulders, and put their faces close together. "Listen to me. This is a hard life. But it's better than what would've happened if we'd stayed. I had to get you out of there."

Liza, who had expected her to shout back, was disturbed. "Why?" she asked in a small voice. "What was so bad?"

Kay looked at the floor. "You'll just have to trust me."

"I do. But I miss Mary Alice. And Mom."

"I know." Kay hugged her. "I'll explain it all when you're bigger." She returned to the stove.

Liza wanted to know now. She got out their plates, forks, and cups and set them on the pantry crate, which doubled as a table. Uncovering the buttermilk pie, she set it in the center. "Would you really have beat up Lee with that baseball bat?"

"If he'd made me."

"He was only playing. You know what a dumb old boy he can be. He didn't even know he'd hurt me."

Kay snorted and stirred the hash with a fork. "What was in that box of books Miz Burger brought?"

So that was the end of that topic.

6

Hobkin

The Burgers stopped by to take Kay and Liza to Sunday dinner on their way home from church—Mr. and Mrs. Burger, Stu, and Mr. Burger's father, who told them to call him Burgie. The three men looked like different stages of the same person, Stu's face showing faintly the same weather lines that crisscrossed Mr. Burger's and marked Burgie's like drought cracks. Stiff and uncomfortable as they were in their Sunday clothes, they trooped into the backyard to see how the goat was doing. Mrs. Burger talked and scratched the spot just between Enid's horn stumps, her poll. Mr. Burger and Stu paced out measurements for a goat pen in the long grass and talked about pasturage, while Burgie stroked his bristly lower lip and was silent. Only as they prepared to go did he say, in a slow, deliberate voice: "You'll have no end of trouble with her if you keep her here by herself."

"Vic told me she wasn't a good goat," admitted Liza, getting into the back of the Suburban.

"Nothing wrong with the goat," said Burgie. "Vic's no good with livestock." He folded his lip as if about to spit; but he had no snuff, and stopped, getting into the front seat between his son and daughter-in-law. "She'll get lonesome. Nothing's ornerier than a bored goat."

At the end of the dusty dirt road, the Burgers' house looked unreal—an ordinary, old-fashioned city dwelling, plunked down with its yard in the middle of the broad nothing of West Texas. A satellite dish watched the plain blue sky from one corner of the yard, and a climbing rose with a single white blossom struggled to shade the porch. Except for the rust-streaked air conditioner on the roof (a swamp cooler, which humidified as well as cooled), it would have been at home in San Antonio; but in the midst of farm buildings and grazing cattle, goats, and horses, it looked foreign. The trailer beyond the windmill belonged to the landscape much more.

"Y'all make yourselves at home while we go change," said Mrs. Burger, leading them into a startlingly cool front room that smelled deliciously of roast beef. "We'll only be a minute."

"Can I go look at the horses?" asked Liza.

"If you want."

"No," said Kay, walking over to the TV as the Burgers vanished. "You'll get all dirty before dinner." She pulled the knob, and the weather channel came on.

Liza wandered around the room. The pictures on the wall were mostly cowboy prints or family photos. Her hair felt funny flopping loose after being in braids so long, and her legs felt naked below the hem of her skirt. "I should've worn my jeans."

"It won't hurt you to dress up once."

"But I can't go tramping around horse lots in my sandals."

"You shouldn't, but I bet you do anyway. How are you supposed to work this? All I get when I turn the knob is static."

"You've got to use the remote," said Stu, reappearing suddenly. Kay jumped as if she'd been bitten. He looked a lot more comfortable now, but Kay eyed him suspiciously. Liza felt vaguely embarrassed. A picture of Stu in cap and gown stood on the table at one end of the couch, and a similar picture of a girl stood on the other end. She pointed to it, and asked abruptly, "Is that your sister?"

"Yeah, that's Sara." Sara. So the name in the book was just coincidence. "She's up in Lubbock taking summer courses." Stu smiled at Liza, bringing out one set of faint facial lines. "I'm going to A and M in the fall. Do I look like an Aggie to you?"

Liza looked him up and down solemnly. She had heard of Aggies, students at Texas Agricultural and

Mechanical University, all her life. Their cowboy boots were labeled TGIF to remind them that "Toes Go in First." Their dogs had flat noses from chasing parked cars; and when a tornado went through the A&M campus, it did over three million dollars worth of improvements. Those were the jokes she'd always heard. It had never occurred to her that it was a real place with real students. "No," she said. "You look ordinary."

"Liza!" said Kay sharply. Stu laughed. Liza didn't understand the reason for either, but it seemed to break the ice.

After a week of isolation, boredom, and hard work, Sunday at the Burgers' was like a holiday. Stu and Mr. Burger knew millions of Aggie jokes. Mrs. Burger cooked a dinner Liza couldn't stop eating and talked about all kinds of things it was important to know about living in the country. She also asked questions; but when Kay gave short, unhelpful answers, she stopped. Burgie didn't talk much; but when he did, everyone else was quiet.

By the time they reached the strawberry shortcake, Liza felt enough at home to ask Mr. Burger, "Can I see your rattlesnake hat pin?"

"Hat pin? You mean hat band?" He wrinkled his eyes at her.

"No. Vic said you cut the rattle off that seven-foot snake to make a hat pin."

"Oh, Vic," said Burgie, as if something had just been explained to him.

"What's Vic been telling you about a seven-foot snake?" asked Mr. Burger.

With a sinking feeling, Liza repeated the story of the snake in the dark. By the time she finished, the Burgers were all smiling. "He made it up, didn't he?" she finished. "I was stupid to believe him."

"Oh, he didn't make it up," said Stu. "He just moved it closer. It wasn't Dad did that, it was some old boy in Junction."

Burgie shook his head. "Naw. Happened thirty years ago. Over in Paint Rock. I think it was Clovis's second cousin."

"Don't look so down in the mouth," said Mrs. Burger, passing Liza the Cool Whip. "Vic wasn't meaning to lie to you. He likes to tell stories, is all. We figure one day he's going to move to New York and write trashy novels that get turned into TV movies and make him millions of dollars."

"I guess he never came to our place at night and met the ghost, either, huh?" Liza did not try to hide her disappointment.

"Of course not," said Kay. "You know better than to believe in ghosts."

"Oh, I don't know," said Burgie. "I don't doubt he drew the longbow a bit, trying to give himself a better reason for bringing back a borrowed horse all in a sweat; but he did have little round bruises on him, just like Nita Stark had that time. That haunt could pinch like nobody's business if he'd a mind to. Or that's what Nita said."

Kay frowned at her plate and looked sideways at Liza, who knew what she was thinking.

"You're as bad as Clovis, Granddad," said Stu genially. "Don't go scaring the poor kid."

"I'm not scared!" protested Liza. "I want to know. Why would the ghost pinch Nita Stark? I thought he liked the family."

"Oh, he did," Burgie assured her. "But Thelma Destry dared Nita to sit up and watch him one night, and he didn't go for that. She came to school mad as a hornet, with tiny round black-and-blue marks on her arms. She wouldn't talk to Thelma for a week. Hobkin'd pinched her till she cried and then undone all her chores, and all Aunt Enid said was she should've known better."

Liza had her mouth full, so it was Kay who said, "Hobkin? Was that the ghost's name?"

"Wasn't it like his nickname or something?" asked Stu. "I know you always call him Hobkin, and so did Aunt Enid, but it seems like the only ghost there could be would be Larry."

Burgie shook his head, scooted back his chair, and removed the snuff can from his back pocket, where it had left a permanent white ring in the denim. "Hobkin was around before Larry died. I remember like it was yesterday, first time I ever went to school. Sissy and me stopped at the Stark place to walk with Ranny and Nita and Mavis, and Aunt Enid was heating up the washing, and Larry was running in and out, and there was the cradle with the baby in it—that'd be Willa—

no, Lionel, Willa came later—the cradle was rocking all by itself. So I went over to see how it did that, and Ranny caught hold of me, and he goes, 'Leave it alone. It's just Hobkin.' " Burgie packed snuff into his lip.

"You never told me about that," said Stu.

"Mph." Burgie got the snuff settled and talked around it. "Maybe if you didn't spend so much of your life staring at that one-eyed monster in the living room, you'd have time to hear what the old folks have to say."

"I'd like to see you get along without your sports channel," said Stu, and turned to Kay. "Y'all ready to look at the horses?"

Liza sat up eagerly, but Kay demurred. "We'll help your mom clear up first."

"That's not necessary at all," said Mrs. Burger. "You go have a good time."

"It's the least we can do after such a good dinner, and we don't mind," said Kay firmly. Liza opened her mouth to protest, met her sister's eyes, and shut up. At least it would be less of a chore with indoor plumbing than it was at home—but there were so many dishes!

By the time Kay let her go, a car full of Guerras had pulled up in front of the trailer. They had been to Mass at the Catholic church and followed it up with dinner at the Rock Hard Café downtown. Vic had three older sisters—one about as old as Kay was supposed to be, one as old as she really was, and one named Hester about midway between Kay and Liza.

Hester and Vic came with Liza to see the horses while the others went up to the house and joined Kay and Mrs. Burger in grown-up conversations. Liza, at Stu's suggestion, got the loan of a pair of Vic's jeans and boots from the trailer. After Stu led her around the corral on horseback a couple of times, he turned them loose to ride and went back to the porch. Liza wished fleetingly, as she followed Vic out of the corral, that Mary Alice were there, then forgot all about her.

It was a wonderful day, if a bit too hot. Back home Hester would have been too old and Vic the wrong sex to be her friends; but out here these differences seemed less important. They saw armadillos, roadrunners, and deer; explored unexpected outcrops and fissures in the apparently flat landscape; drank from stock tanks; and got sunburned. When their stomachs rumbled, they turned back and found a supper of potato salad and leftover roast waiting for them. "You're going to be too sore to go shopping tomorrow," Kay told Liza. "You remember the time you rode the horses in Brackenridge Park?"

"I can ride lots better now than I could then," said Liza. "You think maybe a horse would be good company for Enid?"

"No," said Kay flatly. "No horses."

"But what if there's an emergency? If I had a horse I could ride up here or to the store for help. And Miz Burger said Enid wouldn't keep the lawn short, after all. Enid could eat the weeds and the horse could eat the grass."

"Absolutely not!"

"I had an idea about that," said Stu. "We've got some goat culls up here we set aside to butcher for the Fourth of July barbecue. There's nothing wrong with most of them; they just aren't as good as the ones we're keeping. I don't see why Liza shouldn't have one, do you, Dad?"

"No, thank you," said Kay. "One goat's enough trouble."

"Two goats're less trouble than one," said Hester. "Anyway, you can't keep them in milk all year. Come September La Bruja'll be ready to dry up and start a new kid."

Kay raised several objections; but in the end Liza was allowed to go down to the cull pen and pick out a second goat—a white one, this time, that she decided to call Mavis. Mavis was loaded into a pickup, along with some more goat-care paraphernalia, and Mr. Burger drove them home as the sunset splashed fistfuls of color extravagantly across the sky.

"You like ghosts and things, do you, Liza?" asked Mr. Burger, as the mesquite thickened in the final mile. "You might want to check out that pasture there sometime." He pointed to a rocky field, beyond the barbed wire, to the east.

"What happens there?" asked Liza, leaning across Kay to peer out the window into the distorting darkness.

"Oh, ever once in a while, I'll drive by here late for some reason, and I swear there's a bonfire in that field, with folks dancing around it. But in the morning, there's not a trace."

"Ooh. What if you go look at night?"

Mr. Burger shrugged. "Never tried. See that stone wall just beyond? That's the graveyard."

Liza shivered happily. Squeezed in the front seat between Mr. Burger and Kay, she had no room to be frightened in.

When they turned into the drive to the Stark place, a shadow bounded suddenly into the headlights and stood glaring at them. Kay gasped. Liza grabbed her arm. Mr. Burger put on the brakes. Enid, in the headlights, and Mavis, in the truckbed, bleated. "Reckon she got tired of waiting for you," said Mr. Burger.

"Oh, Enid, you bad girl!" Liza braced herself for a chase through darkness and mesquite; but Enid allowed herself to be caught and led into the pickup without undue trouble.

"She's about ready to be milked," said Mr. Burger, "and glad to see another goat. No, don't worry, goats always bump heads. It's like saying hello." He helped them unload the goats and spread bedding for them ("Ain't good for them to sleep on the ground."), driving the truck around back of the house so they'd have the headlights to work by, then accepted their thanks with ease, and drove off when everyone was settled. He said nothing about Liza's ineptness at milking.

Liza was too tired to go to the trouble of a bath, but she and Kay brushed their teeth at the trough and went together to the outhouse. It was easy to think about ghosts—about Hobkin and mysterious bon-fires—in the bright matter-of-factness of a Sunday af-ternoon, but now Liza was glad to have Kay beside her. The scrub that fringed their domain was full of rustlings and calls; strange shadows fluttered across the white stars. When a pale shape drifted overhead, Liza had to bite her lip and remind herself that it was only the owl.

"You need to be careful what you say to Miz Burger," said Kay, on the way in from the outhouse.

Liza had to realign her thinking with an effort. "Why? She's nice."

"Yeah," said Kay, leading the way into the dark kitchen. "She's a lot too nice for our good. She wants to write to the schools in Amarillo to see if she can find somebody named Willa that would be our great-aunt or our grandma if we were really Starks. If one of the real Starks turns up, we're done for."

"So what did you say?"

"Well, it'd look funny if I said 'No way.' So I said I thought it'd be better if I wrote asking for Willa. I won't, of course, but I can say I did." She sat down on the pantry box and sighed.

Liza got out her bowl and poured some of their remaining cow's milk into it. "Mom wouldn't like it if she knew how many lies we tell every day."

"You let me worry about Mom," said Kay harshly.

Silently, Liza carried the bowl to the back step.

"I don't think there is any cat," said Kay.

"The bowl's empty every morning," said Liza. She

hadn't heard any meows for a while and had begun to think the skunks were drinking it. "I guess it might be Hobkin."

"Oh, Hobkin! This place isn't any more haunted than Lee's house was. When are you going to learn to tell when people are pulling your leg?"

"When I want to," said Liza.

7

Downtown Britt

————————— *Liza did not hear the bats return next* morning. When she opened her eyes, it was already light, and she was too sore to move. She lay listening to Enid and Mavis bawling in the yard, Kay moving around in the kitchen, and birds singing with obnoxious cheerfulness in the mesquite.

"C'mon, Liza," called Kay from the outer doorway. "It's time to milk your stupid goats."

"I can't move," groaned Liza. "I hurt all over."

"You didn't hurt too much to wash the milk bowl and start coffee."

"I didn't do that. Hobkin did."

"I don't have time to play games with you! It'll be a whole week before I get another day off, and if you

can't go shopping today, I'll just have to go by myself.
Don't blame me if you don't like any of your clothes."

Liza dragged herself off her sleeping bag—it had
been much too warm last night to sleep inside it—and
tried to stand up. The attempt made her cry out with
pain. "I told you you'd be sore after all that riding,"
said Kay unsympathetically; but she fetched the tube
of Mentholatum from the first-aid kit in the bottom of
her backpack. She rubbed great greasy gobs of it all
over Liza's legs, back, rear end, and shoulders, and
soon the soreness was replaced by cold burning. Liza
started to cry. She couldn't help it. She hadn't felt this
bad since her ear got infected in first grade. Kay kept
rubbing her, making soothing noises, until the burning
wore off and she could move on her own.

Although it wasn't yet quite eight o'clock, Liza felt
as if she had overslept badly. She milked Enid and
Mavis hurriedly, with the result that more milk went
on the grass than into the bucket. Kay had to remind
her to rinse the egg off her plate so it wouldn't be
impossible to wash off later. Neither wanted to mess
with actually washing the breakfast dishes, and Liza,
for the first time since arriving, did not roll up her
sleeping bag or put her dirty clothes in the washtub.
It was enough trouble just brushing all the knots out
of her hair after yesterday. Between being whipped
around by the wind and then being slept on, her hair
was a tangle that would have made Mom cry to see.
Kay helped her, but in the end they had to cut a couple
of knots out with the nail scissors.

"Sure you want long hair?" asked Kay sarcastically. That was one thing she and Mom had always agreed on—that it was silly of Liza to want hair hanging past her shoulder blades. Kay liked her hair short, and Mom liked hers big.

"Yes, I do," said Liza stubbornly. "I just won't wear it unbraided anymore."

It would have been a long walk into town, but Mr. Guerra waved at them as they passed the store and offered them a lift. Kay accepted grudgingly. He was going to the next town, thirty miles away, to do some business he couldn't do in Britt. "There's a lot of business like that," he told them. "If you took every town in the county and mixed them up together, you might make one good city. We're lucky to have the school here and the movie house. If you're anything but a Baptist or a Catholic you got to drive thirty miles to go to church; and since Miz Leecom retired last year, you either cut your own hair or drive fifty miles."

"How does anybody live here?" asked Kay, looking out the window at drab houses and dusty yards.

"Oh, same way they live anywhere. Most of us were born and raised here. If a place is home, it doesn't matter if it's got a beauty store or not."

Mr. Guerra dropped them at the bank, a two-story building with fancy carvings all around the door. Inside, it was as cold and boring as every other bank Liza had ever been in, though it smelled different, and the teller sat behind a shiny brass cage instead of a counter. While Kay filled out slips and talked about the weather, Liza wandered outside again. The yellowish stone of the bank's outer walls was pocked and spotted with fossil imprints of seashells and trilobytes. Intrigued, Liza walked up and down the front, feeling the crinkly ridges of ancient molluscs. The few people who passed her smiled and said a few words about how she must be "the little Stark girl" before going about their own business.

She was just reflecting on how nice everybody in Britt was, when a young man in a plaid shirt and a dirty Stetson stopped and stared at her. "Oh, you're the other one," he said. "Well! Let me get a good look at you." He stared at Liza till her face burned. She turned away and studied the trilobytes. "Oh. Too big to talk to me, huh?"

"I'm not supposed to talk to strangers," said Liza, not as loudly as she'd meant to.

The man spat tobacco juice. "I ain't no stranger. I'm Randy Phelps. Your sister did me out of a job. Don't know what that makes us, but we ain't strangers."

"Kay didn't do you out of a job!" protested Liza. "You didn't show up."

"Not my fault. Somebody'd been playing tricks on me." He leaned closer to her, and she shifted back half a step. Randy had awfully bad breath. "I don't know how they did it, or who it was, but I was driving back in from Nenupa Creek in plenty of time, and somebody changed the roads on me."

Liza stared at him.

"Don't look at me like that! Everybody thinks I went

over the county line and got drunk, but I swear the road changed on me! I got all turned around—dust blowing everywhere—and I drove half the night and never saw a road sign. So finally I gave up and pulled over on a nice wide piece of shoulder, smack in the middle of nowhere; and when I woke up, I was right in front of a gas station in Childress! Now you tell me how that could be!"

"I don't know," said Liza nervously. Did he blame her and Kay, or what? Fortunately Clovis came along just then.

"Leave the kid be, Randy," Clovis said. "T'ain't her fault you don't know up from down. How you like country living, little lady?"

"It's okay," said Liza. "I got a couple of goats."

Randy scowled at Clovis and walked away. Clovis hung around for five minutes, telling her how worthless the Phelpses always were, before he went on to the drugstore.

Kay came out at last, and they went shopping. This was a very different proposition from shopping in San Antonio. All the stores were ranged around the town square, their broad front windows dusty and a little bare. When Kay and Liza finished in one place, they walked into the hot street again and walked through wind and blowing dust to the next one. Many stores were closed—not just for the day, but boarded up and empty.

One of these had been the beauty parlor. Liza stopped to peer in through the glass door and imagined

Mom presiding over the single barber chair, the single hairdryer, and the sink. Ladies like Mrs. Burger would line up in chairs along the wall looking at beauty magazines and talking about how much they needed rain. Men like Mr. Guerra would come in and ask her for a trim. Kay would be working at the store, so if Mom needed any help with the register, Liza would come in after school. She would—

"Liza, come on! Do you want boots or not?" called Kay. Liza hurried to catch up with her.

Britt had a JCPenney's, but it only had one floor and a mezzanine. There was also one men's store, one ladies' store, and one kids' store; a western wear store; a hardware store; the drugstore; and a Hallmark. At one time there had been a Thom McAn shoe store, but it was closed. Kay got cheap boots at Penney's, but Liza was pickier. The pair she wanted was in the western wear store, red saddle leather with fancy stitching; but Kay said it was too expensive. The saleslady—she said she was Clovis's daughter Ruth Ann—did her best for Liza, explaining that the boots could be bought on time and that they were the year's most popular style. "When the little girls come back from camp, you'll see almost all of them have this kind of boot. And you know what little girls are like!"

"I'm not paying a hundred dollars for boots when she can get them at Penney's for twenty-five," persisted Kay.

"Those had cardboard in them!" cried Liza.

"Remember, she's going to be chasing goats through

the chaparral," said Ruth Ann quickly. "You don't want to take any chances on cheap material, not with the snakes and the cactus. We've got some plain ones here that are all leather."

Finally they settled on an undecorated but sturdy pair in russet, and, rather than carry the box around, Liza stuffed her tennis shoes into a bag and proudly stepped into the street in real western boots. She felt like she belonged here now; and when her feet started to hurt her, she bore it uncomplainingly.

They lunched on hot dogs and butter-pecan ice cream at the drugstore, where Kay bought a box of stationery. "Who are we going to write to?" asked Liza, with a lift of her heart. Maybe Kay had changed her mind about not letting anybody know where they were?

"It's for trying to find out where Aunt Willa is," said Kay out loud; then, more softly, "It's kind of a waste of money, but the way news travels in a town this size, I'd better act like I'm going to write to Amarillo or somebody might get curious."

"Then we should get stamps, too," suggested Liza, recovering from her disappointment and trying to be practical. Kay was right, of course. There wasn't any use in running away and getting whole new identities if you were going to write and tell folks what you'd done.

The number of things they had to buy was appalling—dishes, pans, hooks to hang their clothes on, tools, jeans, shirts, work gloves, and dairy mix to feed to the goats. Everyone was friendly and curious—one lady even invited Kay to join the Baptist choir and gave Liza a form to fill out for joining Girl Scouts—and said how much they had liked and respected Aunt Enid. Liza wondered if they would have been so popular if they weren't supposed to be Starks.

No one was around to give them a lift when they finished late in the afternoon and headed for home carrying their dishes and clothes. The rest would be delivered. Liza's feet were acutely painful in the new boots. "I'm going to fall down in the shade and read when we get home," she said.

"I'm going to climb into a tub of cold water," said Kay.

They walked up the drive between limp-leaved mesquite trees and listened to the locusts warming up for their summer performance. One would buzz, then fall silent; another would start, joined suddenly by others; they worked themselves into shrill intensity, and then stopped suddenly. Scaly Inca doves bounced and pecked in the dust between the weeds, and horny toads scuttled out of shade and into the sun they loved. Liza wondered what was missing.

"What's the matter with those goats of yours?" asked Kay. "Last couple of days Enid's started bawling by the time I got this close."

"Maybe she doesn't need to bawl with Mavis for company," suggested Liza, readjusting the bags she was carrying. Her shoulders and fingers were sore and thick, though less so than her feet, and she was God-awful thirsty. Spitting cotton, as Vic said. What was that on the roof of the house?

"Oh, man!" groaned Kay. "Somebody wrecked the place!"

It did look like that at first glance. Liza's sleeping bag was wrapped around the chimney, and her dirty clothes blew around the yard. Both goats were missing, and the breakfast dishes cluttered the gallery, covered with ants. However, all of Kay's stuff was right where she had neatly put it away that morning; and the only thing amiss inside was the sand drifting in through the open doors. They couldn't remember whether they had taken care to close the doors behind them or not. "I bet it's Vic, playing stupid practical jokes," said Kay. "You go find those goats. I'll see what I can do with this mess."

It was a long afternoon. Enid and Mavis weren't in the mesquite, or in the creek, or along the road. The sun was almost going down, and Liza was ready to cry, when she saw them doing some silly goat dance in the field where Mr. Burger said he sometimes saw a bonfire. Liza wondered how she was supposed to catch them. "Enid!" she called. "Mavis!" She opened the gate, shut it carefully behind her (Vic and Hester having impressed on her the importance of closing gates in the country), and trudged dispiritedly into the field.

To her surprise, the goats bounded toward her, baaing happily. She had wanted to shout at them, but they were so glad to see her, she didn't have the heart. "I ought to turn you both into barbecue, you rotten things," she muttered, taking hold of their chain collars.

"Baaa," said Enid, lipping her T-shirt. Liza led them slowly back across the pasture, pushing their heads away when they got too intimate, scratching them under the chains when they were good. She was too tired even to hold her head up, which was how she saw the arrowhead.

At first she wasn't sure that was what it was. Tiny and perfectly shaped, it stood out dark against the white ground of the cowpath. Enid gently butted her behind as she bent over to pick it up, and Liza swatted her absently. It had to be an arrowhead, even though it was smaller than seemed possible. It was too regular and symmetrical to be natural. "Oh, wow," said Liza, suddenly feeling better. She stuffed it in her pocket, took Enid's chain again, and hurried to get home before dark.

8

Fire in the Night

Once she had been Sara, and summer had been a long, hazy dream of TV, swimming, gossiping with Mary Alice, and reading mystery books. If Sara wanted to leave her bed unmade and her plastic horses undusted, to lie in the backyard listening to the mockingbird, no one would stop her, because Mom, and Lee, and her big sister, Melissa, all worked, and came home too tired to care.

Sometimes Liza missed being Sara. Enid and Mavis had to be milked twice a day, fed their dairy mix, and—after they ate up all the weeds in the yard— taken to some safe pasturage. One day Stu brought her some old bedsprings and helped her make a pen where the goats could sleep without being tied up; another day Mrs. Burger took her to the dump and helped her select materials to make a gate for the drive so Enid and Mavis could sometimes be turned loose around the house and not wander out to the highway. She seemed to be constantly heating water to wash one thing or another. The bats kept the mosquitoes under control, but she had to be alert all the time against fleas, ticks, crickets, and roaches. As each June day went by hotter and drier than the one before, more and more dust drifted into the house, till she had to sweep at least once a day.

If she shirked any little chore, something always happened to turn it into an enormous job. Mysterious winds sprang up to pile sand dunes inside each window. Enid and Mavis got out of their pen and chewed the laundry. Once she put off taking the garbage out, and the skunks came into the house for it. Not daring to approach them, Liza watched in agony as they rolled dirty chili cans all over the house, crushed eggshells, and tore damp paper towels into hundreds of tiny pieces. She began to be careful about doing work as soon as she saw it needed doing, because she knew if she didn't, it would need doing worse in an hour or so. As long as she did that, the jobs stayed small, and they often vanished before she could get to them, as Hobkin heated water or swept in one room while she was busy in another.

Sara had read only when it was too hot or dark to play, when Lee was hogging the TV, or when the mood happened to strike her. She had liked stories and comics about girls who did exciting, unusual things—solving mysteries, living with animals, coping with the dangers of the wild frontier. Now that Liza was, more or less, involved in all these things herself, she read for information and for a chance to rest.

The handbooks told her all sorts of things she might need to know at a moment's notice, like how to recognize rabies or set a broken leg. The horse books showed her how country girls were supposed to act and talk. Sweeping the floor went much faster if she had a head full of knowledge, because she could plan how to use it in any sort of situation. If, for instance, she and Vic ever had a fight and Vic fell into the creek and broke his leg, she knew exactly what she would say and do. The fairy encyclopedia and the Nancy Drew books seemed beneath her now, but Aunt Enid's diaries told how life was supposed to be lived on the Stark place. They also gave her clues about Hobkin.

Liza made one serious attempt to explain to Kay about Hobkin. Tired to death of Frito pies and canned pasta, she had studied the cookbook, walked down to the co-op for the necessary ingredients, and cooked hamburgers and pinto beans for supper. The beans were inedible, because she had decided to be really economical and pioneering and get dried ones, not realizing that they had to be soaked overnight; but the hamburgers came out more or less all right. Kay ate them appreciatively, though they were a bit cold by the time she got them, Liza having cooked them a little too early.

"Y'know, when I think how hard it used to be to get

you to make your bed, I can hardly believe you're the same girl," she said, as she put the dishwater on to heat.

"I'm not," said Liza. "I'm Liza now."

Kay laughed. "Oh, is that what did it? Anyway, I'm proud of you. When we left home, I had my mind made up that I'd have to work doubly hard to take care of you; but ever since we got here, you've taken care of yourself just fine. If I didn't see it right in front of me, I wouldn't think it was possible."

Liza had been wishing Kay would take some notice of how hard she worked, but now she felt obscurely guilty. "Well—it isn't possible, really," she said. "I couldn't do it without Hobkin."

Liza waited for Kay to say there were no such things as ghosts. Instead, she scrubbed out the bottom of the frying pan with a paper towel, and asked, "Oh? What does Hobkin do?"

"Well—first, he doesn't let me be lazy. If I'm supposed to do something and I don't do it, he makes it worse. You, too. If you hadn't forgotten to cover the milk last week, he wouldn't've spilled it all over the icebox."

"Oh, that was Hobkin's fault, was it?"

"No, it was yours for not covering the milk! He did it to teach us a lesson. Even doing my level best I still can't get everything done, so he helps. He always washes the cat bowl. Lots of mornings I get up, and the floor's already swept. And I don't make your coffee in the morning; he does. And today I washed the jeans and towels; but when I left the hamburgers cooking to go see if the clothes were dry, he'd already folded them and put them where they belong. And when I got back, he'd flipped the hamburgers for me, and you could tell they'd been flipped just in time to keep from burning."

"Is that all?" Kay sounded particularly grown-up, with an edge of amusement that bothered Liza.

"Isn't it enough? I *think* he might be making sure Enid and Mavis come when I fetch them in—but they just might have figured out when milking and feeding time is, all on their own."

"Oh, it might as well be Hobkin, if you like to think that." Kay slid her hands into oven mitts and took the water from the stove to the drainboard. They washed the dishes in a dutch oven full of hot water and rinsed them with a saucepan full of cold.

"It doesn't matter what I like to think," said Liza. "It only matters what's true!"

"Look, if you want to make up imaginary friends and tell stories to pass the time, that's fine. You have to act grown-up so much, it's no wonder you feel like being babyish sometimes. But I don't want you turning into a liar like Vic."

This, from the person who had faked their birth certificates and invented the whole story of their connection to the Starks, was too much! "Vic's not a liar, and neither am I! There really is a Hobkin! You can read about him in Aunt Enid's diaries if you don't believe me."

"One of these days I'm going to give all the old men

in Britt a piece of my mind," said Kay, rinsing their cups. "Can't you see it's just a story, to make life more interesting? Probably Hobkin was a hired man or an uncle or something. Whoever he was, he's not here now, and it's not funny trying to make me think you think he is when you know perfectly well it's impossible."

"But—"

"I don't want to hear any more about it," said Kay, in a voice Liza couldn't argue with.

Liza couldn't sleep that night. For once the wind had ceased to blow, and the only sounds in the darkness were the sneezing of the owl, the squeaking of the bats, the faint rustles of animals about their own business. Even sprawled stark naked on top of her sleeping bag, no part of her body touching any other, with all the windows open as high as they would go, she was as hot as if she'd been shut up in an oven.

Finally she went to the door between her room and Kay's. It was darker here, and hotter, but she could hear the deep, steady sound of her sister's sleeping breath. Back home they had shared a room, and when a sleepless Sara had heard that sound from the other bed, she had known that it was safe to slide open the bolt with which Melissa shut the door each night and creep out about her midnight business. The house and yard had been more exciting by night, the simple act of getting cookies out of the jar suddenly dangerous. Melissa had warned her once that Lee was likely to mistake her for a burglar and shoot her dead. Sara had gotten out of bed even more often after that.

Sara's thrills seemed cheap and babyish now, but it would be cooler outside. Not intending to go far, Liza slipped on her sandals to protect the soles of her feet from the prickly grass and then her sundress to keep her from feeling silly for wearing shoes but no clothes. Walking carefully so as not to wake Kay, she stepped through her outer door.

Colorless in the dark, a low, doglike shape put its front paws on the edge of the trough and bent its head to drink. Liza's heart stopped. Coyote! No—if it were something dangerous, why were Mavis and Enid quiet? Anyway, it seemed small for a coyote. She watched it drink, trying to pick out its shape from the similarly colorless shapes beyond it. Slim body— bushy tail—it raised a sharp nose and pricked-up ears momentarily toward the sky. A fox! There was an honest-to-goodness fox in her backyard! As Liza held her breath, it dropped back on all fours and trotted away, into the scrub behind the barn.

When she was sure it was gone, Liza went to the trough herself, drank, and splashed water on her face and arms. She did this several times a day now, either at the trough or with the melted icewater in the drip pan under the icebox. It was a big help in desert country with no air-conditioning. Her dark shadow moved on the water, and a pale shadow drifted up to join it with a dull grating sound.

Liza jumped. "*Kschh!*" sneezed the barn owl, its claws rattling against the metal on the opposite rim of the trough. Its flat, white mask of a face was too close to hers, its beak too big, its claws too long. Involuntarily she jumped back. It spread its wings and relaunched itself into the air, drifting in a circle above her head like its own ghost. Oh, she was such an idiot! She'd been within arm's reach of a wild animal, and then she'd gone and scared it!

"*Kschh!*" sneezed the owl contemptuously, and drifted over the house. She ran around the corner after it, following without thought or hesitation down the drive, over the improvised gate, and up the road.

The owl soared across the stars and out of sight. In the pasture behind the graveyard, a bonfire blazed from the earth to the moonless heavens, shadows dancing like goats around its light. Liza ran to the fence, kicking dust inside her sandals, and stared through the barbed wire. Because of the distance and the inconstant light, the only thing she could tell about the dancers was that they seemed to be upright and waving their arms, moving in rhythm to each other and to a pulselike beat that vibrated from her feet to her eardrums.

The barbed wire (bobwire, people here called it) was meshed too close to crawl through. Liza let herself in quietly by the gate. It was hard to walk in silence, with rocks cropping up suddenly out of the dust and grass to twist her sandal and bruise her heel. She and Vic had explored this pasture one long, hot afternoon, looking for more arrowheads, playing Comanche. She had seen a roadrunner run away with a baby rattlesnake dangling from its beak. The thought made her curl her toes. "Rattlesnakes sleep at night, dummy," she reminded herself. She could hear the drums that made the pulse in the ground and voices chanting abrupt, meaningless syllables.

Remembering a maneuver that had allowed her to scalp Vic in the Comanche game, she dropped to the ground and crawled, alternately on her belly and on her hands and knees. Sundress and sandals were less effective than jeans and boots had been, but she felt safer, less conspicuous.

Although the bonfire roared halfway into the sky, the pasture did not get hotter and she smelled no smoke. The figures, oddly, seemed smaller the closer she got to them. Every now and then the movement around the fire would pause while one figure broke loose from the circle and did a solo dance. Once it was a shuffling, crouching step, close to the ground; once, a wild, high-jumping performance; once, a bobbing dance like the movement of an Inca dove. Mostly the figures were silhouettes, but sometimes a tongue of fire would bring out a flash of color—red, brown, or black—a man's glistening bare chest, a fringed buckskin knee. They're Indians! thought Liza, crouching behind a creosote plant fifty yards away; and then, as her confused eyes pulled all the sights together and made a picture of them, They're midgets!

Only they were too small even for that. The smallest grown human person she had ever seen a picture of was not much less than two feet high, but these could not be more than a foot high! She was about to wiggle closer when the circle paused again for another solo, and the strangest figure of all capered into the light.

It was taller than the others, wearing a long shirt instead of Indian britches, shaggy, ragged, and out of place. The rhythm changed subtly, and the newcomer danced a different sort of dance, singing in thick, strange English:

"Hobkin cross the ocean, Hobkin cross the sea,
Finger worked to bone, and nae rest for me,
For the acorn's not yet fallen from the tree
That'll grow the wood to cradle the bairn
That'll grow the man to lay me."

"Hobkin!" squealed Liza, sitting up.

The light went out.

The wind rose.

The night filled with the pounding of tiny running feet and the shouting of shrill voices.

Liza remembered Nita Stark, black and blue because she'd spied on Hobkin one night and he'd pinched her till she cried. Liza leaped to her feet and began to run, but they were already on her—dozens of teeny-tiny invisible fingers all over her bare arms and legs and cheeks, tweaking her toes, reaching under her skirt. She ran faster, tripped on her sandals, fell sprawling, flailing with her arms and legs as they pinched, pinched, pinched! She knocked off the one that was on her chest, twisting her nose, but the others pinched harder. She could feel their mocassins slipping on her skin as they scrambled to sit on her, weigh her down so they could pinch her to death! It was like that last time Lee had held her down and tickled her—but Kay would not hear her if she roared this time; and even if she did, what could Kay do against hordes of invisible Indians?

"Hobkin!" screamed Liza, tears flooding down her cheeks and into her mouth. "Hobkin! I didn't mean to spy! Honest! I'm sorry! Hobkin! Call them off! Please! Hobkin!"

9

The Encyclopedia

_____ *Something snatched her up, and the* pinchers fell off of her one at a time, clinging furiously as she hurtled through the air, across the pasture, over the fence. The last one dropped as she skimmed the tops of the first mesquites. Liza was too terrified to scream, for the hands that held her up were as invisible as the fingers that had pinched her, and the ground looked farther away than it should. "Ho-Hobkin?" The only word she could manage came out half-whisper, half-sob.

"Howd thy tongue!" said a rough voice in her ear as they swooped down to her window. Hobkin set her on the sill, letting go so suddenly she bumped her head on the pane. Shaking, she let herself down into her room and stood waiting, but apparently Hobkin was done with her for tonight. She blew her nose and scrubbed her face with Kleenex—not daring to revisit the trough to wash—undressed again, and crawled, heat or no heat, inside her sleeping bag.

By morning, round, blue bruises covered her arms and legs. She was hot, headachy, dirty, and tired. When she heard the bats come home, she got up to wash herself in soothingly cool water. The owl sat in its loft door, preening its wings, and watching her. Liza stuck her tongue out at it. "Go away, you nasty bird! This is all your fault!"

"*Kschh!*" said the owl, then began the horrible hacking noise that always preceded its coughing up a pellet of undigested hair, bone, and fur from its night's meal.

She scrubbed out her sundress in the last of her bathwater, hoping not to have to explain last night to Kay. The skirt had several tears in it, and dirt was ground in, back and front. Enid and Mavis bleated to be milked.

Kay was cooking bacon when Liza brought in the milk and the morning's water. "Good morning," said Kay brightly, taking the bucket; then she suddenly turned fierce. "What happened?"

She had noticed the bruises, thick and blue below Liza's sleeves. "I'm sorry," said Liza.

"Whoever did that is the one that'll be sorry! What'd he use? A board with nails in it? Who did this?"

"Nobody," said Liza.

Kay studied her face. Liza realized she must have bruises there, too. "Whoever it was, he doesn't deserve your protecting him! No matter how nice he seems the rest of the time, if he beats up on people smaller than him, he's the lowest thing on the planet! And don't be scared. I won't let it happen again. Was it Vic? Or Stu?"

"It wasn't anybody! Honest!" All idea of trying to explain about Hobkin and the little Indians fled. Kay would think Liza was covering up for somebody and go around accusing people of beating her up. She decided on as much truth as she could get away with. "I couldn't sleep last night. I didn't mean to go anywhere—honest—but the owl came real close, and I got interested and followed it out to the pasture. But there wasn't any moon, and I got nervous and tried to run and fell down one of those dry gulches. There's thousands of little rocks, and I think I hit every one of them on the way down. Nobody hit me."

"Cross your heart?"

Liza nodded and crossed her heart solemnly. "And I spoiled my sundress, too."

"Well, if you were running around in the middle of the night, you only got what you deserved." Kay let go of her and turned the bacon. "But you remember what I said about people hitting on you. Nobody's got the right to do that. If anybody tries, you grab the frying pan or something and hit them right back, and then come running to me."

"Nobody wants to hit me," said Liza, putting a paper filter in the mouth of the clean glass milk container they'd bought at the feed store and pouring the milk through to strain it, a little at a time. She was getting better at this, but still spilled milk from time to time. "But sometimes people deserve to be hit, you know."

"I'm the only one around here with any right to decide if you need a spanking or not. And nobody deserves to be hit hard enough to raise a bruise. Are you okay now?"

"I've got a headache."

Kay lifted the bacon onto a plate covered with a paper towel. "Better get you an aspirin. And take it easy today. I can pasture the goats on the way to work."

The aspirin did not work fast enough. After Kay departed leading Mavis and Enid, Liza washed the milk pail and the breakfast dishes and felt worn out. Maybe Hobkin wouldn't mind if she read for a while before she dusted. She didn't know what business it was of Hobkin's, anyway. She wasn't sure whether she was mad at him for being so bossy and particular or grateful to him for saving her from the little Indians. She wondered if he had pinched her, too, before she apologized.

When she looked over her books, she found she didn't want to read about horses and country living and useful things. She wanted something absolutely different from the reality she was living. The romance novels looked boring. Mom read them sometimes, but Kay said they were silly. Liza had already read one of the Nancy Drew books back home, so she picked up the other, but the headache got in her way. She couldn't read more than a paragraph at a time; and by the time she reached the end of a page, she had forgotten what had happened at the beginning of it.

Liza decided to try the *Encyclopedia of Fairies*. It was divided up into entries, seldom as much as a page long, and she could skip around in it, looking at pictures and reading whatever caught her attention. Some of the words were funny, because they were spelled phonetically in British dialects—"bairn" for baby, "cauld" for cold, "tha" for you. She found she could work it out all right most of the time; and when she couldn't, she read a different entry. Locusts buzzed. Birds chirped, darted after flies, hopped about pecking at the long, dry grass. The windmill creaked. Liza slumped against the crate in the shade of the gallery, her bottom flat against the ground and her bootheels digging comfortable notches for themselves as she propped the book against her knees and idly turned the pages.

Goblins. Golden hair. Selkies. Lutey and the Mermaid. The Cauld Lad of Hilton, wailing a pathetic song:

> "Wae's me, wae's me;
> The acorn's not yet
> Fallen from the tree
> That's to grow the wood,
> That's to make the cradle,

That's to rock the bairn,
That's to grow to a man,
That's to lay me."

Liza sat up, remembering Hobkin's song, forgetting
her headache. The Cauld Lad of Hilton was described
as half-brownie, half-ghost. He had done kitchen
work, tidying up what was left messy, and messing up
what was left neat. The servants of the place where he
lived made him a green cloak and hood, so he changed
his song and disappeared.

Holding her breath, Liza turned to the H's. There
was no entry for Hobkin, but she found "Hob, or
Hobthrust," "Hobgoblin," and "Hobmen." She read
eagerly. These entries again mentioned brownies and
also referred her to "Lobs and Hobs," on the way to
which entry she ran across one on the "Little People
of the Passamaquoddy Indians." When looking for the
part about brownies, she accidentally found a description of bruises just like the ones all over her now, left
as the result of fairies pinching someone who spied on
them!

She read, flipping from one part of the book to
another, until she stopped running across new descrip-
tions of familiar things. Then she sat back, breathless
and dizzy. Brownies were fairies who attached themselves to people or places, guarding them and doing
house- or fieldwork until someone made them mad or
laid them with a gift of clothes. Sometimes they played
tricks on people, punishing them for laziness or bad

manners. They lived on milk, and sometimes bread or cake, left out for them by the people they helped. In the north of England, brownies were called hobs. Nobody knew where they went when they were laid, but one possibility was that they joined the ranks of the trooping fairies, who lived underground and came up at night to dance. Some brownies had been known to follow English people to other countries when they moved, but the book didn't say much about that. At least one tribe of Indians up near Canada told stories about fairylike beings.

"But it's so stupid," Liza said to the horny toad eating ants in the sunlight two feet away. "Nobody believes in fairies!"

She looked at the writing in the front again. Aunt Enid must have had some reason for giving a book about fairies to Sara Burger. It was hard to imagine either the hardworking, practical woman who had written the diaries or the girl in the graduation picture—now studying to get her degree in agriculture as quickly as possible—caring about imaginary little people. Yet, there was nothing flimsy or Tinkerbellish about the brownies in the book, or about Hobkin, or the Indians. The people who told stories about brownies in England were the same sorts of people who lived here, farmers and cattlemen and so on. Why was it easier for her to believe in ghosts than in fairies?

Liza made soup for lunch, read the book while she ate, then rinsed her dishes and dusted, thinking hard. The book was mostly about English fairies, but it described a lot of what went on around here. The section on being pixy-led even matched up with what had happened those times Vic and Randy Phelps had gotten lost. She had never heard of Indian fairies, but she didn't know much about Indians; and if people lived on both continents, fairies might as well, too.

Hobkin must've come from England with Aunt Enid and made friends with the natives. After she died, he stayed and looked after the Stark place, which explained why it was in such good shape when they got here. He had chased out people, who would have messed the place up; but he had made her and Kay welcome. She wondered what they had done to deserve it. Maybe he only liked girls or maybe he knew that they needed a place to stay. Maybe he had pixy-led Randy Phelps that night just so Kay could have a job and they didn't have to run away any farther!

Suddenly Liza laughed. He had pretended to be a cat so he could have milk at night again! He must have been awfully hungry if he hadn't eaten since Aunt Enid died. Even now, milk by itself wasn't much to live on. She stopped in the middle of dusting Kay's windowsills to fetch the book and look up what fairies ate.

As soon as she finished dusting, she studied the cookbook and decided the most acceptable thing she had ingredients for would be oatmeal cookies. Kay was always complaining about how much she spent on snacks, anyway.

Liza was taking the last cookies out of the oven when Stu showed up. Lately, whoever drove down to the mailbox in the afternoon would stop in and see her. She watched his face carefully as he ate the cookies she gave him. "It's scorched on the bottom," she said. "I didn't have a timer."

"It's only a little burned," he assured her. "Want me to help you scrape that part off?"

He took half and scraped them at the drainboard. Liza scraped the other half on the pantry crate. He wanted to know about her bruises, so she told him the same story she had told Kay. She was trying to figure out how to lead the conversation around to Sara, Aunt Enid, and the fairy book, when she heard the goats coming and Kay yelling for help.

Stu dropped the knife and cookie he held and ran to the door. Liza followed more slowly, pretty sure she knew what the matter was. Sure enough, Stu started laughing. Kay had lost hold of Enid, who was bounding happily all over the yard, and Mavis had decided to eat a mesquite tree, to which end she was standing on her hind legs, ignoring the red-faced Kay hauling on her chain. "Don't just stand there, give me a hand with these stupid things!"

Stu caught Enid, and Liza helped drag Mavis to the pen, where the goats at once settled down, rubbing their long, soft hair—which would someday be mohair and bring in cash—against the bedsprings to comb it. "You're still not used to animals, are you?" asked Stu, laughing, as Liza measured out the dairy mix.

"That's no reason to make fun of me," snapped Kay, retucking her shirttail.

"You'll feel better after you have some of Liza's cookies."

Kay snorted. "Liza, don't forget to wash your hands."

"Say," said Stu, "I was wondering. You and Liza don't get out much. You want to run into town and see the movie tonight?"

"That movie showing now was in San Antonio three months ago. It'll be fall before y'all get a movie I haven't already had a chance to see."

"Probably, but you can see a movie twice just to get out of the house, you know. It'd be good for you. Life in the boonies can drive you stir crazy."

"We're fine, thank you."

The tone of Kay's voice embarrassed Liza. "Kay likes it this way," she said, to detract from her sister's rudeness. "She never went out at home, either."

"Kind of hard on you," Stu said to Liza. "Good thing the girls'll be coming back from camp in time for the Fourth of July. You'll have somebody to play with besides Vic and the goats for a change."

After he left, Kay turned unexpectedly on Liza. "I told you not to let any boys into the house while I was gone!"

"But that was ages ago!" Liza protested. "Stu's all right. You know that!"

"I don't know anything like that at all!"

"It would've been weird to make him wait outside while I brought him a cookie."

"What did you have to offer him cookies for?"

"What on earth's the matter with you?" demanded Liza. "I can't even be neighborly without you jumping on me."

"You made me a promise, and you broke it. Don't let it happen again."

Liza was about to argue some more when she remembered that the book said fairies gave bad-tempered people cramps. She shut her mouth tight and fetched the milk pail.

10

The Fourth of July Picnic

——————— *By the time the Burgers picked them* up on the Fourth of July, Liza was a nervous wreck. She climbed into the back of the Suburban clutching for dear life the potato salad she and Hobkin had made (Hobkin had kept the potatoes from boiling over and saved the mayonnaise jar when she dropped it). She had braided her hair three times but still had one fat braid and one skinny one. Her jeans were stiff from being newly washed yesterday, and she wore her best blouse—yellow, with pearlized buttons. Her first attempt at saddle-soaping her boots had not made as much difference as she thought it should; but Hobkin had apparently gone to work on them during the night, and they looked as good now as when she'd walked out of the store.

"You all ready to meet the other girls?" asked Burgie, as she buckled her seat belt. "You look mighty nice."

Liza swallowed. "I guess so."

Mrs. Burger looked over her shoulder. "I think the other girls are going to mostly wear sundresses."

"Liza destroyed her sundress chasing owls," said Kay. Her hair was still damp from washing, drying rapidly into little curls around her face. The ugly hairdo was growing out, and she looked nearly pretty this morning.

"Will all the girls my age be there?" asked Liza.

"Most of 'em," said Burgie. "All the Baptists and Catholics, anyway. The Church of Christers and the Pentacostals've got a long drive to their picnic."

"I wonder if that teacher's little girl will be there?" said Mrs. Burger, as they turned onto the highway. "We got this third-grade teacher last year, who never even tried to go to church, plus he's divorced, so he almost didn't get to stay on. Only he was such a good teacher, he finally got that Burkhard girl passed to the fourth grade; and after a miracle like that, even the hardshells had to admit it'd be a shame to lose him."

Mrs. Burger talked all the way to the picnic grounds on the other side of town. Away from the highway, Britt was a pretty place in its way, with frame houses that had probably been built originally with the proceeds from cattle drives and added on to, a room at a time, during good years. Most people were trying to grow shade trees or flowers; and, though some of them had not painted their houses in Liza's lifetime, others had done their best to brighten up the landscape by painting theirs yellow, blue, pink, or green. Liza could tell which houses belonged to no one. Their windows were blank and dusty and their yards parched jungles of mesquite, tumbleweed, and Johnson grass.

The picnic ground, marked off by hedges of sage, a cedar-lined creek, and the low gray walls of grave-yards, lay between the two churches on the other side of town. Salads and desserts already crowded long tables in front of the aisles of booths. From enormous barbecue grills by the creek rose the thin, white smoke of mesquite wood striving to attain the correct temper-ature for cooking goat meat. More people were gath-ered here than Liza had seen since coming to Britt.

Vic came running up while she put her potato salad on the table, between a Jell-O mold and something made mostly of orange slices and coconut. "Hey, 'bout time you got here! Come play the dart game. Hester's running it. And you got to get some fireworks. Don't buy them from Mr. Arnold; they're duds. Mr. Montez has the good ones."

"Can we set off fireworks here?" asked Liza, follow-ing him.

"Sure! We're outside the city limits." In proof, he jerked a string of firecrackers out of his pocket. "Only be careful where you let them off. Last year, this guy set off a Roman candle under Father Santillian's chair, caught his robe on fire—man! I thought he was going to get excommunicated!"

Compared to Fiesta in San Antonio, the Britt Twelfth Annual Interdenominational Fourth of July Picnic was a pretty poor show, but Liza was in no mood to be picky. The games were mostly things like darts and ringtoss, though the Baptist senior class had improvised a skeeball booth. Bits and pieces of "Pop Goes the Weasel" haunted the field all day as Ruth Ann stopped and started the tape for musical chairs. The prizes were mostly small, but half a twenty-five-cent ticket bought a sizable cup of lemonade, and three whole ones bought a small assortment of fireworks.

Soon Liza spotted the girls her age. As Mrs. Burger had predicted, all wore sundresses—white, yellow, and blue—with pastel plastic sandals. After a month at Girl Scout camp, they all had the same dark brown skin, Mexicans and Anglos set apart only by their hair. The Mexicans had long, loose, black tresses tumbling down their backs; while most of the Anglos had shorter hair, bleached and frizzy with sun. Half a dozen girls hung out by the skeeball, with not one pair of boots, jeans, or braids in evidence.

Vic had run off to the dunking booth, where someone he knew had taken his turn on the dump seat. Liza dawdled by the lemonade stand, watching the girls. They jostled each other for turns at skeeball, cheering as a tall girl in a blue sundress scored a hundred fifty points. The sun beat down on Liza's head and shoulders, pressing the fabric of her blouse and jeans against her body. Her boots felt too large and heavy. Two of the girls began a clapping game, chanting

"I woke up Sunday morning,
And looked upon the wall.
The beetles and the bedbugs
Were having a game of ball."

Liza took a swig of lemonade and walked over, fingering the tickets in her pocket. She had as much right to play skeeball as anybody. She hovered at the edge of the group, trying to smile in a friendly way, when one of the girls turned around and saw her. "Hi," she said, through a mouth as dry as if she'd never tasted lemonade. "Is this the end of the line?"

"Over there," said the other girl shortly, pointing at the smallest one in the group. The girls not otherwise occupied looked at Liza. The clapping girls clapped faster.

"I'm singing eeny-meeny and a miny-mo,
Catch a whipper-whopper by his toe—"

Liza took up her place as indicated, keeping the smile fixed where it was. "I'm Liza Franklin. My sister and I came to live on the old Stark place."

"Yeah, we heard about y'all," said the tallest girl, in a slow, deliberate voice. "We heard you were goat ropers."

"I've got two goats," said Liza, glad of this opening, "and there's skunks under the house, and—"

"Oooh!" The tall girl wrinkled her nose and pulled

an elaborate face. "No wonder it smells so bad all of a sudden."

The shortest girl covered her mouth and turned away, but the others laughed straight at Liza. The clapping girls stopped clapping to laugh, and the girl playing skeeball stopped in the middle of her windup to look her up and down. "Goats and skunks both!" she said. "That's the worst combination I ever heard!"

"My goats don't stink!" Liza exclaimed. "And the skunks don't, either, not if you don't bother them, and I don't!"

The skeeball crashed against the backboard, missing every ring. "Look, she stinks so bad she spoiled my shot! Let's go get fireworks!" The girl collected a plaid stuffed dog, and they all ran off, the shortest girl last, looking over her shoulder. Probably regretting that she hadn't had her turn at skeeball! Liza clenched her fists and glared after them, her face burning.

"Don't pay any attention to them!" said the teenage girl in the booth. "They're being stuck-up because you're new in town. Give them a couple of weeks, and they'll be friends all right."

"I wouldn't want to be their friend, anyway!" said Liza, less clearly than she meant to. "I bet none of them could take care of a goat without it stinking! Mine don't. I keep them clean."

"There isn't one of them could take care of a house by themselves like you're doing, either," said the teenager. "I talk to your sister when we go to the store, and she's always bragging on how clean you keep the house and how you're learning to cook, without even any water or electricity. I bet they're mad because their mothers have been talking about you every time they forgot to make their beds since they got back from camp."

"I bet you're right!" said Liza fiercely, but she still wanted to cry. Instead she played skeeball, hurling the ball with such force it kept bouncing back out of the rings, and all she won was a little bag of potpourri.

Every time she saw the cluster of girls the rest of the day, Liza turned around and went in the other direction, even when she was with Vic and he called her a chicken. She was late to the goat barbecue, even waiting till all the girls had gotten their plates and sat down before she got in line. Vic was already going back for seconds when she joined Kay, the Burgers, and the Guerras at one of the long tables by the creek.

"You having a good time?" asked Kay.

"Okay," said Liza, putting her bag of prizes on the table between them. "I've got three stuffed animals and a Texas flag. And look, here's a game of checkers I got in the fish pond. We can play checkers in the evenings now." She cut up her meat, and mixed barbecue sauce in her pinto beans. "I feel funny about eating goat. I mean, it might've been Enid."

"You'll get used to that," said Mrs. Burger. "Country folks can't afford to be sentimental."

"You'll feel a lot better about it once you taste it," Kay assured her. "It tastes just—"

Bang! Bang! Pop! Bang!

101

The explosions almost lifted Liza off the bench. A moment's silence, as the whole picnic stopped talking, was followed by nervous laughter and indignant shouts. Liza thought she saw a blue skirt vanish behind a cluster of grown-ups, but she ground her teeth together and said nothing. It was no good telling anybody. She didn't even know the girl's name. Later on, when it started to get dark and people were settling down for the fireworks, she'd take a whole bag of fireworks and she'd sneak up behind the girls and she'd light them all at once and throw them right in the middle of their mean little group!

A man who had been pointed out to her as Reverend Burns, the Baptist preacher, stood up on the end of a bench. "All right now! Whoever threw that, step forward!"

He asked three times, without result, before beginning a lecture about firework safety. Liza had never heard such a voice before. Every word he said rang out clearly over all other sounds, without any microphone. He told about the time he had thrown a cherry bomb under somebody's chair to see him jump, and how that person had gone to the hospital and nearly died, pulling through only after the reverend—who hadn't been a reverend then, just a little boy—stayed up all night praying and begging God to make it come right. From this he swung into talking about careless sins and how hard it was to stay right with God and your fellow man. Kay leaned across the table to Mrs.

Burger. "Not exactly what I'd call a good dinnertime topic," she whispered.

Stu laughed. "Old Burns does this every year! Sooner or later somebody's bound to do something stupid with a firework, and he can't pass up the chance to preach. Nobody's ever got hurt yet."

"They will someday, if they don't stop selling the fireworks," said Mrs. Burger. "Every year there's a handful of us mothers that wants to shut Mr. Arnold's firework stand, but that would mean all that business would go to Mr. Montez and the Catholic Sunday school would get the money."

"It's the same way with us," agreed Mrs. Guerra. "Till we both decide not to have them at the same time, they're going to both keep selling fireworks."

"What's the point of the Fourth of July without fireworks?" asked Burgie. "Sixty-five Fourths I've seen, and never saw anybody hurt bad by fireworks, yet."

"I think it's pretty nice of Arnold and Montez to sell them at the picnic and give the Sunday schools the money," said Stu. "If the churches didn't let them sell here, they'd set up booths on the road and keep the money."

Kay's face flushed red. "That's just like a man! What good is all the money fireworks ever brought in if a kid gets hurt? What if those firecrackers had landed in Liza's lap?"

They got into a grown-up argument, and Liza went for seconds. The goat meat really did taste good.

Maybe she should stroll by the table where the girls were eating and accidentally-on-purpose dump a plate of barbecue down that blue girl's back. She wished Hobkin had come. He would've fixed them!

She pondered her revenge the rest of the afternoon without ever fixing on a good one. At dusk she bought a fistful of sparklers from Mr. Arnold (who was not selling duds; that had been Vic drumming up money for the Catholics), still planning. After that she forgot her anger in the pleasure of chasing through the dark trailing streamers of multicolored sparks. The sky-rocket display was not as varied or as long as the one she usually went to at Fort Sam Houston, but Mr. Arnold and Mr. Montez competed with each other in setting them off, and the result was better than she would have expected in a town this size.

Only when she was alone again in her dark, hot room late that night did she think about the other girls. People did pick on new girls at home—a bit—she'd done it herself—but those firecrackers—! They'd done it because they knew she was all alone. Nobody that counted would help her out. Vic was a boy, and it didn't matter what boys did; and Kay was the same thing as a grown-up anymore. If only she'd had Mary Alice! She and Mary Alice had done everything to-gether—played, fought, watched TV, gone swimming. They'd even run away together once, when they were little. Mary Alice had broken a window and asked Sara to run away, too, to keep her company.

Had she hurt Mary Alice's feelings by not asking her

to run away with her and Kay? Liza hugged the stuffed bear she'd won, feeling guilty and anxious. Mary Alice didn't know how firm Kay had been about telling absolutely no one. She was probably mad at Liza right now—only she didn't even know about Liza. Mary Alice and Sara had never had secrets.

Feeling that she no longer had any friends anywhere in the world, Liza began to cry.

11

Friends

————————— *Liza forced herself to do her chores* the next day, though she couldn't see the point of them. Nothing stayed clean in this land of endless, dry wind; and who cared if she kept a clean house? No one would come to see her. Nobody liked her. The furniture wasn't worth keeping clean for its own sake—just a bunch of crates and an organ that didn't work! They weren't living here, they were camping out, and Kay seemed all set to camp out the rest of their lives.

Nevertheless, Liza went through the motions. No telling what Hobkin would do to her if she didn't. Stupid, bossy brownie! Who did he think he was? He was worse than any grown-up. Work, work, work, all the time, and never so much as a game of checkers. (That they hadn't had any checkers till the day before did not lessen her feeling of being put upon. Kay should've provided them before.) She would get old before her time. She would work herself to death, and the town girls would bring flowers to the grave crying with guilt because they'd said she stank. Hobkin would huddle miserably at her headstone. Kay would wear black and repent, at length and in great detail, making her delicate little sister run away to such a hard life. Mom and Lee and Mary Alice would show up—how would they get here?

Liza was working out a plausible way to get people from San Antonio to Britt for her funeral, when she found herself dusting the grit off the pad of stationery Kay had bought. The paper, envelopes, and stamps still sat unused. What a waste! Kay was too cheap to buy furniture that they'd use every day, but she was willing to throw money away on something she knew she'd never need, just to make her lies look more real.

Well, Kay wasn't the only person in this house who could write. Liza had a pencil around here somewhere. She could write to—whom? She had promised Kay solemnly never to give anyone any clues about where and who they were now, but she didn't have to put a return address on the envelope. She could write to Mom, but Kay said Mom didn't care about them anyway. Lee was more important to her than her own daughters. You could tell by the way Mom backed him up no matter how stupid and unfair he was. She had even let him flush the goldfish Sara had won at Fiesta that spring down the toilet.

Liza shied away from the memory of that scene. No, Mom didn't deserve a letter and probably didn't want one. On the other hand, she really owed one to Mary Alice. She should never have let Kay drag her away without saying good-bye. Liza stopped feeling sorry for herself and started feeling guilty for deserting her best friend. She had to write and explain, no matter what Kay would do to her if she found out!

By the time Liza found a pencil, sharpened it with her pocketknife, and settled down on the gallery, using the seat crate as a table, guilt had given way to concentration. She had to explain very clearly, without giving anything away. Mary Alice wouldn't tell on her, but her mother was the sort of person who opened all the mail as soon as it came in, whether it was addressed to her or not. It took Liza the rest of the morning, and the rest of her eraser, to write something satisfactory.

Dear Mary Alice,

I know you're probably mad at me, and I don't blame you. I'm writing to explain as well as I can, but Melissa has sworn me to secrecy so I can't tell you anything that will let anybody know how to find us.

Melissa has planned for us to run away as long as I can remember. She learned how to make new identities from TV and a book she ripped off from the library (only she returned it when she was done with it and

108

paid the whole fine. Melissa lies something awful but she's not a thief). We aren't Sara and Melissa Welch anymore. I can't tell you who we are, but I'll give you a hint: I won't have to sit in the back of the room at school; in fact, if we were in the same room, we would be together.

I have been keeping this secret from you since right after Fiesta. You remember Mom was working evenings all spring, and I was mad at Lee for flushing my goldfish. So one day Melissa was making supper and I was bored and Lee wanted to make up. He brought me that plastic horse I'd wanted so long and some of those expensive chocolate truffles. So I sat next to him and he started horsing around and tickling me. Only you know how dumb Lee can be, he wouldn't stop tickling me after it stopped being fun and was holding me down tickling under my T-shirt and I was screaming and howling and kicking and even started to cry but he wouldn't stop and I couldn't get away. So then Melissa came in and she had a baseball bat, and she made him stop. She told him if he ever put a finger on me again she'd beat him black and blue, and then she took me in the kitchen and said as soon as school let out, we were running away. She made me swear all kinds of secret oaths, on a Bible and everything, and that's the only reason I didn't tell you.

Anyway, I can't tell you which direction we went, but we live in the country in a haunted house. It's really truly haunted, but not by a ghost; if you were here I'd tell you all about it because I could prove it but it's kind of hard to believe so I better not tell you. The haunt is a big help with the housework, which is good because I have to do it all. Melissa is working at the only ice house which is also the bus station, only buses don't stop but once in a blue moon. This is a little place and if you don't like what her boss has in his store you've got to drive thirty miles, also if you want to get your hair done. The grown-ups are nice but the girls are mean and I don't have any friends, just the haunt and this boy that lives five miles away. I miss you, and Mom; but Mom didn't love us, anyway, or she wouldn't always be on Lee's side, Melissa says. I have two goats, but they do not stink. We live like pioneers with no electricity and drinking goat's milk.

By this time Liza's fingers were stiff, and she was having to squeeze words at the bottom of the back of the paper. She signed her old name, addressed the envelope to Mary Alice Fraga in San Antonio (but she couldn't remember the zip code), and walked down to the mailboxes. Stu had helped her straighten the Stark mailbox and repaint it with the name Franklin, but it had never had anything in it but cobwebs. Uncertain whether Kay would be able to see that the flags were up from Mr. Guerra's store, she laid her envelope in the Burgers' box on top of the outgoing stack of mail.

It was close to lunchtime, but Liza wasn't hungry. She hadn't finished dusting, but there wasn't that much more to do. She didn't want to go back, but she also didn't want to go to the store, and that only left the graveyard in walking distance. Her boots raising puffs of white dust, she walked along the shoulder of the road with her head down, kicking a rock before her.

The graveyard was ragged with burrs and Johnson grass, the white and gray gravestones tilted and cracked. No one had been buried here since the new churches were built on the other side of town, right after World War II. Liza always thought of graveyards as spooky, but this one was hot and shadowless under the noonday sun. Horny toads scuttled across the names of long-dead Burgers and Arnolds. Inca doves bounced in the sunshine. A jackrabbit bounded up and flashed across her vision from a thicket of Johnson grass to the gray line of the wall. In places, the grass was trampled and the weeds torn away from the stones, as if goats browsed here sometimes.

Liza went from headstone to headstone, peering at the inscriptions from underneath her hatbrim. Some were almost impossible to read, pale white words etched on pale white stone; others had been cut deeper, and the same drifting dirt that marked the cracks between her floorboards filled in the letters and made them stand out. *Baby Ferguson—Jan 1898–Feb 1898. Sophie Ann Burger, 1854–1872. Victim of Comanches. May her soul find peace with God.* Criminy, the Burgers had been here over a hundred years! She tried to find Guerras, but found no Mexican names at all. The old-time Catholics must have had their own cemetery.

Most of the gravestones were newer than those two,

but several were dated 1918—old people and young, men and women, all in the fall and winter. She wondered what had happened that year. People of the same name tended to be clumped together; and she found the Starks, after some searching, with young mesquites springing up among them. The Starks had been around almost as long as the Burgers. The earliest stone was for a two-year-old who died in 1883. The biggest was for Annabel Fortune Stark and Burnet Stark, who died within three days of each other in November 1918. The most recent was a low limestone marker, nearly hidden by Johnson grass, for Lawrence Lindbergh Stark.

"Larry," whispered Liza, and began hacking away the grass with her pocketknife. *1927–1932. Son of Rankin and Enid Gutch Stark.* Liza touched the date gently. Five years old. Unexpected ideas rose wordlessly in her as she stared at the stone. Since 1932 there had been no rattlesnakes on the Stark place. That must be Hobkin's doing. Why hadn't he done it before then? Did he feel like it was his fault that Larry never lived to grow up? And how had Enid felt about it? She had ended the diaries in 1929, and the stone gave no clue.

The sound of wheels on gravel distracted her. Raising her head, Liza saw a girl with brown arms and a brief, sun-bleached ponytail propping a pink bicycle against the graveyard wall. It was the shortest girl from the group yesterday—the one who hadn't gotten to play skeeball. She took a thermos, a bag, and a table-cloth out of her bike basket.

Liza froze between her options. She could bound away, like the jackrabbit, over the back fence and into the bonfire field. There wouldn't be any little Indians in the daytime, and it didn't make sense to stay here and be picked on. On the other hand, why should Liza let some stupid, nasty girl chase her out of anywhere? She stood up, and demanded, "What do you think you're doing?"

"Oh!" The girl jumped as if she'd been hit, took a firm grip of her bag, and faced her. "I'm having a picnic."

"That's disgusting," declared Liza. "Having a picnic on top of all these dead folks."

"I wouldn't mind if somebody had a picnic on top of me when I was dead," said the girl unexpectedly. She didn't sound like most people in Britt; something about the way she made her vowels and the way she emphasized syllables. "I'd think it was friendly."

Liza stepped forward. "What do you know about friendly?"

The girl looked at Liza's boots. She had boots on herself, the same fancy-stitched ones Liza had wanted. "Oh. You mean yesterday. I didn't want to be mean. I know what it's like."

"That makes me feel lots better."

"Shut up a minute so I can apologize! Yesterday was the very first day that bunch ever let me hang around with them in town. See, at camp we were all one troop, all us girls from Britt, and we hung together. Nobody that wasn't from Britt could pick on me. So I thought maybe now things would be different. I was having a good time, and then you came along, and DeAnn said you stank and Leti said that about you throwing her aim off, and they were all laughing, and it was funny when you answered what she said about goat ropers with that about skunks."

"I didn't see anything funny about it!"

"That's because you aren't from around here. Around here saying you're a goat roper is the same as saying you stink."

Liza's face started to burn. How was she supposed to know something like that?

The girl sighed miserably. "Anyway, it didn't help. Later on they called me Cow Patty just the same. And when I told Leti I'd tell on her about the firecrackers, she said they'd all swear it was me. And they would, too."

"Aren't there any nice girls in this whole town?" asked Liza.

"Not really. There's this one Church of Christ girl that at least talks to me, but all she ever thinks about is Jesus." Her voice turned bitter. "Dad says they're all right underneath and once they get used to me things'll be fine, but I think a whole year is enough time to get used to somebody."

This connected up with what Mrs. Burger had said

yesterday. "Is your dad that third-grade teacher who's divorced and doesn't go to church?"

"Uh-huh. I'm Patty Maguire. I'm from Houston."

"I'm Liza Franklin from San Antonio."

Somehow the fact that Patty was also from a city made Liza more inclined to forgive her. They sat on the wall with Patty's picnic (iced tea, grape jelly and raw hot dog sandwiches, Bar-B-Q potato chips) between them, comparing notes. Patty thought the mixture of lies and half-truth Liza had to tell her exciting and romantic. She herself had been perfectly happy in Houston, but her father had gotten nervous when their apartment was broken into, and he took a pay cut to come to Britt. "He said we'd have fresh air and safety," she complained. "He didn't mention being bored out of my gourd."

"Why do you have picnics in the graveyard?" asked Liza.

"I like graveyards. They're private. And I can't stay in the house all the time. It's a pretty good house, and we don't have to pay rent, but it wasn't lived in for a long time and Daddy's fixing it up. I've been sleeping on the back porch all summer because my room's torn up."

"Don't you help?" asked Liza. It sounded kind of fun to her.

"Sometimes. But there's lots of heavy stuff I can't do." She sighed and threw the crust of her sandwich into the grass for the birds. "There's a chicken shed out back, but Dad won't let me get any. He says I can have one of our neighbors' kittens."

"I'm thinking about getting chickens next year," said Liza, which was true, in a way, for it suddenly seemed a good idea. "And we need a cat. I always wanted one."

"You know what I heard?" asked Patty, licking her fingers to pick potato chip crumbs off the tablecloth. "I heard the old Stark place is haunted."

"It is," said Liza, finishing off the tea, "but it's nothing to worry about. Not if Hobkin likes you."

"I thought his name was Larry."

"That just shows what people in town know about it." Liza dusted crumbs off her jeans with a superior air. "Larry was only five when he died. His ghost couldn't keep the place clear of rattlesnakes and help with the housework like Hobkin does."

Patty eyed her suspiciously. "You're pulling my leg."

"You can think so if you want. Are you still hungry? We could go up to my house and make a Frito pie, and I could show you the goats and things."

Patty hesitated, and Liza was afraid for a minute she would say no; but then she slid off the wall, and said, "Okay. You can ride my handlebars."

12

Goat Roofer

Liza and Patty heard the commotion when they reached the drive. Mavis and Enid bawled, Vic shouted in mixed Spanish and English, and metal banged. "What is that?" asked Patty.

"I don't know, but we better hurry," said Liza, jumping off the handlebars to open the gate.

Enid was on the roof. She danced on the tin slope, bleating down at Mavis, who ran back and forth below bleating up at her. The Burgers' old horse, Jughead, peacefully cropped the Johnson grass, reins looped over his neck, and Vic shouted. When he saw the girls he changed his target. "There you are! What'd you go off and leave them alone around the house for, you dummy?"

"I didn't feel like taking them all the way to one of

the Burgers' pastures," said Liza. "They're okay here usually. How'd she get up there?"

"She couldn't have," declared Patty, propping her bike against a gallery pole and looking at Vic suspiciously. "Not without help."

"Well, I didn't help her," said Vic. "I was supposed to exercise Jughead, anyway, and I rode over to see if Liza wanted to get back at Leti. Mr. Montez always has a few fireworks left. We could show her what it's like to sit on a firecracker."

"You knew about that?" said Liza in surprise.

"Of course I did! I saw her."

"Why didn't you tell somebody?" demanded Patty.

"Why didn't you?"

Mavis gave up bleating at Enid and ran to Liza, rubbing her with the stumps of her horns and crying, "Maaaa!" Liza patted her neck. "Anyway, it doesn't matter," she said, "not while Enid's up there. We've got to figure out a way to get her down."

"She won't come for food," declared Vic. "I tried an apple I had and a carrot out of your icebox, and she just laughed at me. So then I threw some rocks, but she didn't care about that, either. And Mavis kept getting in my way."

"The first thing is to put Mavis up, then," said Liza, slipping her hand into the white goat's collar. "Come on, honey. Back in the pen for a while."

"We can't lift Enid down," said Vic, as Liza led Mavis around back. "Even if she'd hold still, it'd take two of us, and there'd have to be two people to catch her."

"We've got to go about this rationally," said Patty, in a schoolteacherish voice. "If we can figure out how she got up, maybe we can reverse the process."

"Goats can jump pretty high," said Vic doubtfully, opening the makeshift pen gate. "But I never saw one jump as high as that. You think maybe the haunt put her up there?"

This was just what Liza had been thinking. Maybe Hobkin was telling her it was a bad idea to leave the goats alone in the yard. She was too busy getting the protesting Mavis safely penned to say anything before Patty spoke up.

"Oh, don't be dumb," said Patty. "I never heard of a ghost doing things like that, and I've read a lot of ghost books. We've got to scope out the situation."

The three made a circuit of the house, studying routes to the roof. At least that was what they were supposed to be doing. Liza, knowing what the house looked like, barely looked at it, trying to think of ways to get Hobkin to bring the goat down. Enid danced and slid noisily on the tin roof, baaing. Liza's head began to ache.

"I get it!" said Patty, pointing. "See, she climbed on the woodpile, and then to the top of the lean-to, and then it was just a step to the roof!"

"That's not a lean-to, that's the bathroom and the water heater," said Liza.

"I don't care what you call it. It's the only way she could get up."

Vic studied the arrangement critically. "Yeah. Yeah, she could. Lucky she didn't break her leg on the woodpile."

"That pile's practically all one piece," said Liza. "All the wood's rotting together and the weeds are growing up and tying it in a bundle. The first night we were here Kay had to really work to get enough logs out to cook with." Good, maybe this wasn't Hobkin's fault, after all.

Patty put her hands on her hips and frowned at the house. "Okay. Now we know how she did it. How can we use that?"

"I guess I'll have to go up after her," said Liza.

Patty squeaked. "You'll break your neck!"

"Maybe not," said Vic. "It's not much bigger a risk for her than it is for Enid."

"Anyway, she's my goat and if I'd been here watching, she wouldn't be up there." Liza strode forward and put her foot on the woodpile.

"Hold it!" cried Vic. "You try to go up there in boots, you will break your neck! Go put your tennis shoes on."

"Oh. Right." Liza hurried into her room. The clatter of Enid's hooves above was deafening in here. She pulled off her boots, socks and all, and stuffed her bare feet into long-unused tennis shoes. She felt oddly light and cool as she ran out again and scrambled up the stack of mesquite logs. Some were as big around as her leg and soft with rot; others were just the right size for a switch, shifting under her weight.

Suddenly, the job did not look as simple as it had from the ground. With her feet braced on the topmost logs, she was only about three feet up, and the bathroom roof was a couple of inches lower than the top of her head; but everything felt taller. She would have to pull herself up by her arms, mostly. Liza felt the edge of the roof experimentally. The gutter was rusting, and drifted with old mesquite pollen. The tin vibrated under Enid's hooves. Metal glinted where a layer of rust and dirt had been scraped away.

"What's the matter?" asked Vic.

"You need a boost?" asked Patty.

"I'm fine," lied Liza. "She did come up this way. I can see where her hooves skidded." She took a deep breath and spat on her hands. If an ornery old goat could do this, she could, too!

She had to try three times, pulling with her arms and pushing off with her feet, first off the woodpile and then off the wall. Going up the corner where the kitchen met the bathroom proved easiest; she could brace herself against two walls at once. A mighty shove that sent gray paint flakes and pollen showering into the woodpile got her high enough to put her elbows on the bathroom roof. It seemed to her that the whole house shook, and Enid bleated anxiously.

At last Liza crouched on the bathroom roof, feeling weak in the knees and elbows. If she fell from here she would probably break something, and she would have to lie on the ground and hurt while Vic rode for help. She wondered if Patty knew anything about first aid. And what if—what if she really broke her neck? There wasn't any first aid for that. If you broke your neck, you were dead or maybe paralyzed.

"You okay?" asked Patty.

Liza looked over the edge at their worried faces and wished she hadn't. "Piece of cake," she said, making herself smile. "Maybe y'all should back off. We don't need Enid landing on you."

Vic and Patty took two or three steps back. Liza got her breath and wiped her sweaty palms. She wished those goats would shut up! She knelt on the bathroom roof with her hands on the hot metal of the main roof, and called, "Enid! Come on, girl! Stop being silly!"

"Baaa!" said Enid, braced on the rooftree.

Liza had no choice but to go after her and lead her back. Fortunately the slope was gentle, and the roof ridged at regular intervals; but the tin was too hot after half a day of July sun to put her bare hands on for more than a few seconds at a time and gradually began to burn her even through the knees of her jeans. Enid came when Liza tugged her collar, however, picking her way delicately as her sharp hooves slid on the metal. A couple of shoves, and she hopped from roof to roof to woodpile to ground, where she danced sideways and ran to the trough.

"Ack!" cried Liza. "Get her out of our drinking water!" Vic and Patty ran to catch her, and Liza scooted from roof to roof, then, glad to be done, dropped to the woodpile.

She landed with a wobble, fell on her behind, and the stack, weakened by all the traffic, gave way. Liza gulped. Patty screamed. Vic ran toward her. Logs scattered and invisible arms seized Liza around the waist, hauling her halfway across the yard.

Patty screamed again and Vic stopped dead, just before a large log rolled through where he would have been if he'd kept running. Liza sprawled in the grass, gasping. "Idiot bairns," muttered Hobkin; but when she reached for the sound, he was gone.

Patty bent over her. "Are you okay?"

"I—I think so." Liza sat up, testing each limb. She was shaky and breathless but uninjured.

Vic looked down at her accusingly. "You flew!"

"I didn't. Hobkin did." She got up with Patty's help. "If I could fly, I wouldn't've had to climb, would I?"

"Who's Hobkin?" asked Patty. "What happened?"

"The ghost," said Vic. "The ghost helped her out." He spat disgustedly. "I don't know why he couldn't've gotten Enid down himself, if he can carry people around like that!"

"I bet he would've, if we hadn't been able to manage," said Liza, dusting her jeans. "He likes people to do for themselves before he helps them. And he's not a ghost. He's a brownie."

"A what?"

"You mean—like a fairy?" Patty's eyes had gone very round. "But—that's silly. Nobody believes in fairies except little kids!"

"Aunt Enid believed in them," Liza retorted. "She brought one from England with her. And there's American kinds, too. You know that bonfire Mr. Burger sees sometimes?" Vic nodded. "I saw it, too, only I wasn't too chicken to go look at it, and I saw Hobkin dancing with a whole bunch of little Indians, about yea high." She held her hand grass-height from the ground.

"Oh, right." Vic strode to the trough and dragged Enid out of the drinking water. "I bet they had wings and wands and things. Give me a break!"

"No, they looked just like Indians, only tiny. And— you remember the time I had bruises all over? They did that. They saw me spying on them, and they all went invisible and held me down and pinched me. Hobkin had been dancing with them, but he rescued me that time, too, when I said I was sorry. You saw those bruises. They were just like the ones Hobkin gave you last Halloween, weren't they?"

"Yeah. But so what?"

"So whoever heard of a ghost pinching people? But fairies do it all the time to people that snoop in their business. Come inside and I'll prove it to you."

Vic and Patty pored through the fairy book as Liza fixed Frito pie and told them about Hobkin's behavior. Gradually and grudgingly, Vic was won over; but he remained obstinate about the Indian fairies till Patty fixed him with a hard, bright gaze and said, around a mouthful of grease-soaked corn chips, "You're just jealous 'cause you didn't see them. Liza's story is better than any of yours, and you can't stand it!"

"It isn't fair," he grumbled. "I've been here all my life, and I never saw this stuff. And why didn't you tell anybody?"

"Some people don't have to blab everything they know," said Patty.

Liza drained her milk glass. "Those Indians probably don't want anybody talking about them. If I went around telling people, they might come after me, and I'd rather die. You be glad there was only Hobkin to deal with that time you came here. It's awful to be held down and pinched and pinched all over and not be able to do anything about it!"

"Okay, I can see that." Vic rubbed his arms as if remembering how they had hurt once. "But everybody knows about Hobkin, anyway. You could've talked about him."

"I tried telling Kay. She thinks I'm playing baby games. And it doesn't seem right to talk about things to other people that I don't talk about to her." Liza stared at the chili in the bottom of her bowl. "Always at home, she wanted to know everything that went on with me. If I got in trouble or had a problem, she wanted to know all about it; and if she could fix it, she would. And she still worries about me. She worries way too much; it's a pain. But she doesn't listen to me the way she used to. Half the time she doesn't even believe me." It was as if Kay had gotten so used to lies that she didn't expect the truth anymore.

"My dad's like that, too, since Mom left," said Patty. "I mean—he believes me, but he doesn't always pay attention, and it's hard to get him to understand things. I've told him and told him about the other girls calling me Cow Patty and Shortstuff, but he doesn't get it. He tells me to ignore them. How am I supposed to ignore every girl my age in the whole town?"

"You should call Leti 'Tallstuff,' " suggested Vic. "I never saw such a beanpole."

"Hey!" Patty exclaimed. "You think Hobkin could do something? About Leti and the other girls?"

"I don't know," said Liza. "I don't think he likes to leave the house."

"Well, but if we could get them over here—"

"That's a dumb idea," said Vic firmly. "It's your own fault they pick on you. You don't fight back."

"I do, too!"

"You do not! You get mad and yell at them. That just makes them feel big." Vic stood up. "You want to go get a cherry bomb? I got a real good plan for that. I can get Leti out on the porch to tell her something— my mom's been wanting to borrow her mom's sewing machine, anyway—and y'all can sneak around her pomegranate bushes and roll the bomb underneath. She won't suspect anything because boys aren't usually on any girl's side. What do you think?"

"I think it's a great idea!" Patty leaped to her feet. "Let's go!"

"I've heard worse," Liza conceded, "but we have to wash the dishes and put the goats to pasture first. Hobkin hates it when I go off and leave the dishes!"

13

Busyness

Liza was not bored once during the entire month of July.

Most days Patty rode her bike out after lunch and stayed or took Liza back to town till suppertime. About once a week Leti or DeAnn would commit some outrage against one or the other of them, so that some afternoons were devoted to revenge; otherwise, she and Patty just hung out together.

Girl Scout meetings also happened once a week. Kay complained about the expense of dues and uniforms but paid up promptly. She seemed to understand about the necessity of Girl Scouts better than she had understood about the necessity of boots. Feuding was suspended during Scout meetings, and some of the lesser girls were friendly for whole half hours together. However, Leti Mendoza and DeAnn Holcum, the girl who had called Liza a goat roper, never spoke to the new girls during Girl Scouts; and the other girls were not ready to offend these two by being friendly at any other time.

Patty's father went out of his way to pick Liza up for Scouts and often let the girls and Vic help him fix up the house by laying the tile or painting trim. He never seemed offended when Kay refused his invitations for her and Liza to eat supper at the Rock Hard Café, where he and Patty ate most of their meals.

He had no objection to Liza coming over to watch TV, but the effort was pointless. Without cable or a satellite dish, the Maguires could only get two stations. However, Patty and Mr. Maguire had a lot of books, which they let Liza borrow one at a time and in which she could look up all sorts of important and interesting things. Patty even, in one book about Comanches, found a mention of the Indian fairies. It didn't say much, just that they were called *nenuhpee*, had arrows that always killed ("My arrowhead!" squealed Liza, glad they had only pinched her and not used their bows), and were dangerously powerful, best avoided.

Hobkin continued to make Liza look good to the grown-ups. Vic had lots of ideas for projects, which he confidently expected to be able to put through with Hobkin's help. Liza kept pointing out to him stories in the encyclopedia about fairies who disappeared because they resented being taken for granted. She was sure it was asking too much to get Hobkin to help them build a bat tower, move the bats into it, and clean out the barn so they could ask the Burgers to let Liza take care of Jughead in return for riding privileges.

Not all of Vic's ideas were so extravagant. One day he brought the swingblade with which his dad mowed the scanty grass around the trailer, and he, Patty, and Liza cut the long grass around the house till they were worn out. Then they leaned the blade against the barn and turned their backs to drink lemonade for a while. Soon they heard the swish of metal through grass on the other side of the house. When they looked over their shoulders, the blade was gone.

Patty shivered, smiling. "Weird! You reckon we could see how he does it—kind of casually look around the corner?"

"Not if you don't want to go home with bruises all over," said Vic. "He's nasty when he's spied on."

"And he might go away," added Liza. "I couldn't get along without Hobkin."

By the time Kay came home that night, the yard was almost unrecognizable. The grass, though uneven and ragged around the edges, barely came up to her instep. Due to the wash water daily dumped around the house, a bleached green still tinged the yard, though the country all around was mostly yellow. The house looked more like a real place where people lived than it ever had before.

"What on earth did you do?" asked Kay, collapsing on the gallery and dropping the plastic grocery bag in the dust.

"Vic brought his dad's swingblade over, and all of us worked all day," said Liza. "Looks good, doesn't it?"

Kay frowned. "I can't believe his dad loaned you kids a swingblade. You might have cut your feet off!"

"Well, we didn't." Liza kind of thought Vic had not bothered to ask permission to borrow the blade, but if she mentioned that, Kay would say something mean about Vic. "Doesn't it look good, though? We won't have to pick so many stickers out of our jeans, and the goats and I won't pick up so many ticks. And the cuttings are so long, we can dry them and use them for goat bedding."

"It was a good idea to borrow something to cut the grass. I should've thought of it myself. But you should have waited till Sunday or Monday and had me do it." Kay frowned tiredly. "It's hard to believe you cut all this in one day. You're going to be sore tomorrow."

"I don't get sore as easy as I used to." Liza took the groceries inside, spread out the ingredients on the drainboard, and started preparing fried chicken according to the cookbook. She had already screwed up fried chicken twice, even with Hobkin helping; but chicken was cheap. Liza never knew whether she would produce something edible or not. When she did, she ate it and liked it; and when she didn't, she and Kay laughed and fed it to the skunks. They picked what they wanted out of the cookbook in the morning, and Kay brought back what they needed at night, along with a can of something in case of disaster. If there was no disaster, they saved the can. Kay had had to bring home two new crates and stack them to make a new pantry, once Liza started getting the hang of cooking and using the cans up more slowly.

When the flour coating on the chicken was brown, Liza covered the frying pan, checked her watch, and went out to join Kay on the gallery. "I need to put the biscuits in and start cooking the corn in thirty minutes," she said. "Don't let me forget."

"I'll try." Kay smiled at her absently, the breeze blowing ragged ends of hair across her face. "You want to play checkers?"

Liza trotted into her room for the set, and they sat on the ground, with the board between them on the crate. Mom had taught them to play checkers. It was the only game she had the energy for after working all day, fixing dinner, and doing whatever housework her daughters had left undone. The three of them had played endless round-robin games, the one who sat out last playing the winner, while the TV ran in the background. Sometimes Lee had played, too, but he only lasted till he lost the first time, and then he would either go look at TV or run out for a drink. Liza moved her first checker and said, carefully, "It's almost Mom's birthday."

Kay was quiet a long time, then moved a checker. "So what?"

Play became rapid and careless. "So. Shouldn't we send her a card or something?"

"I don't see why."

"I don't see why we shouldn't. We don't have to put the return address or our new names on it."

"The postmark would show what part of Texas we were in."

"Oh." Liza hadn't thought of that when she sent her letter to Mary Alice. She made a stupid move that lost her three pieces at once. "I don't get a birthday party this year, do I?"

"I'm afraid not. Liza Franklin's birthday was before we ever left San Antonio."

"It's not fair."

"A lot of things aren't fair." Kay brushed her hair out of her eyes with an abrupt motion.

Liza took one of Kay's pieces and concentrated on playing as well as she could. She lost, and set up another game. "Miz Burger's going to town Monday to get her hair done. She wants to know if we want to come, too."

"I don't need my hair done."

Yes you do, thought Liza. Mom'd cry if she saw you. But all she said was, "We could look at the stores, and Miz Burger says there's a swimming pool."

"Now that would be nice! We haven't been able to use our swimsuits once." Checkers slid back and forth upon the board. "I wish we could do something nice for Miz Burger. We owe her for the goats and the books and having us up to dinner every Sunday."

Suddenly Liza had a wonderful idea. "We could fix her dinner. Her and Stu and Mr. Burger and Burgie could all come here for a change, and I'd cook. And we could play horseshoes. Vic found a stake and horse-shoes in the back of the barn."

Kay frowned. "I don't know. We couldn't invite them and all the Guerras; there isn't room."

"The Guerras always eat in the café, anyway. Y'all could play horseshoes while I'm cooking, and then when the Guerras come back from Mass and dinner, the Burgers can go home. I could have dinner almost ready by the time they get back from church. Please? I can cook real good now. You know I can."

"Real well," Kay corrected absently. "You cook fine for you and me, most of the time, but what if it doesn't work? We can't throw it out and feed them ravioli!"

"I'll do it right! I'm sure I can!"

"Well—give me time to think about it. I'm too tired to decide anything right now."

The chicken turned out edible, if a little tough, and the biscuits, cooked according to the instructions on the can, were only a little overdone. I'm obviously getting the hang of this, Liza thought, and there wouldn't be any problem fixing dinner for six people. Roast beef looked simple. She'd fix roast beef. The hard part would be dessert. Liza baked a lot lately so Kay wouldn't have to spend money on snacks and so she'd have something besides milk to give Hobkin, but she'd have to go some to compete with Mrs. Burger's strawberry shortcakes and buttermilk pies.

Kay washed dishes while Liza brought in Mavis and Enid, milked, and penned them for the night. Liza had gotten good at milking, but Enid wasn't giving as much as she used to. Liza'd have to ask somebody about that. Afterward, Liza stood with the covered pail at her feet, admiring the short grass and the vivid sunset. The owl sat in his window preening his ghostly wings. The bats rustled, nearly inaudible under the shush of wind in the scrub and the creaking of the windmill. Kay staggered out with the wash water and hurled it over the short grass. "Hey!" said Liza. "I haven't washed the milk bucket yet!"

"Sorry. You ought to do that in clean water, anyway, not in greasy chicken water." Kay set the dutch oven on the back step and stretched backward, hands in the small of her back. "Ugh! I'm tired! I don't know where you get all this energy of yours. Housework, goat farming, Girl Scouts, and now you want to play hostess! When would you want to do that?"

"Sunday after this one," said Liza promptly.

Kay straightened and looked at her, her expression indistinct in the dusk. "That's Mom's birthday."

"So?" said Liza, folding her arms.

The owl sneezed, and the first bat fluttered into the night.

14

Burgers for Dinner

_____ *Kay and Liza sat on the gallery peel-*ing potatoes and scraping carrots. Enid and Mavis had been banished to the bonfire pasture, so the only sounds were the buzzing of locusts, the creak of the windmill, and the occasional, heat-weakened call of dove or mockingbird. The smell of roast hung on the air, a hearty, Sunday-morning smell. They took the vegetables from a bowl, peeled them over the colander, rinsed them in a bowl of water, and stacked them in the final bowl. Kay rubbed the hair off her forehead with the back of her hand. "I told you we should have gotten canned vegetables."

"That would be cheating," said Liza, struggling with the potato peeler. She wished she had the knife, but

Kay had sharpened it that morning and wouldn't let her touch it.

"It would be a lot simpler and probably come out better," said Kay. "Look, the ones we peeled are turning brown already."

"Just around the edges. And they'll get brown in the pan, anyway."

"Aren't you tired? We've been cooking since we got up this morning."

She was, but she wasn't going to tell Kay that. "I've been cooking. You've been helping."

"Don't be snotty."

Liza stretched the crick in her back. "We're almost done, anyway. This is the last thing."

"I thought you wanted to frost the cake."

"Oh. Yeah. Except that. You think it's cool yet?"

"I don't know. Even if it's room temperature, that's still pretty hot." Kay cocked her head. "Great. Here they come already."

Liza squeaked and peeled faster. The Burgers' Suburban drove slowly up the drive. She was scraping the last carrot when the engine stopped. "Good morning!" called Mrs. Burger, holding a Tupperware cake dish in front of her. "Are we early?"

"No," said Kay, throwing dirty water over the grass. "We're running late. Liza decided she needed to bake a cake this morning, too, and it slowed us down."

"Oh, good, two cakes!" said Stu, pulling a card table out of the back of the van.

"Sure smells good," said Mr. Burger.

Mrs. Burger carried her cake into the house behind Liza, who carried in the vegetables. The starlight cake she had baked that morning sat, rather lopsidedly, on the drainboard. Mrs. Burger put her Tupperware next to it. "My! You've been busy as a beaver."

"I hope it came out okay," said Liza, opening the oven and wincing at the blast of heat on her already-hot face. "I should've made it last night, but I didn't think it'd take so long to put together. Is it cool enough to frost yet?"

Mrs. Burger put her hand on the leathery, uneven top. "Not yet. Why don't we put it on the windowsill? What's the matter?"

Liza had dumped the vegetables into the aluminum roasting pan and was looking in uneasily. Shouldn't there be more juice in the bottom than that? She tried to remember how Mom's roasts had looked at this point, but she had never paid much attention when Mom was cooking. "It doesn't look right somehow."

"Let me see." Mrs. Burger tapped across the floor and looked over her shoulder. "Better put in a little more liquid." She looked at her watch and frowned. "Oh, shoot. I hate these digital watches. They start going weird on you, and there's nothing you can do about it. Is yours okay?"

Liza nodded, running to dip water out of the bucket and wet down the roast and vegetables before covering them with aluminum foil. It was eleven-thirty-five now. At twelve-thirty-five the roast would be done. She and

Mrs. Burger went outside, where Mr. Burger drove a tall stake into the ground while Kay held it steady, and Burgie and Stu argued about the proper length of a horseshoe pitch.

Kay had been doubtful about horseshoes, but it was the only entertainment they had for so many people. Burgie, it turned out, had been horseshoe champion of Britt back in his salad days and had once won a twenty-five-dollar war bond at a county competition. Kay and Liza had never played before; but no one was in practice, so they weren't as outclassed as they should have been. Even at short range, Liza was pretty hopeless; but Kay had naturally good aim, sharpened by playing video games at the Stop 'n' Go back home. "You got a pretty good wrist," Burgie told her approvingly, "for a girl."

Kay stuck her jaw out at this sexist limitation.

Stu groaned. "Granddad!"

"S'matter?" asked Burgie, surprised. "She does. Little practice, she'll be almost as good as you. Strength doesn't matter so much in horseshoes, you know. I've known lots of girls that gave the men a run for their money."

"Don't pay any attention to him," said Stu to Kay. "He's old. He can't help it."

Kay swung the hand that held the horseshoe slowly back and forth, ignoring him. "I don't think I need as much practice as all that," she said, looking straight at Burgie. "I bet I can pitch horseshoes as well as any old man."

Burgie spat out his old dip of snuff and carefully loaded his lip with a new batch. "We'll see about that, little lady."

After that, the others played and kept score; but the real competition was between Burgie and Kay. They played with a calm and deadly seriousness, never smiling, hardly speaking, like the golf pros in the endless tournaments Lee used to watch.

Burgie started out with a clear lead, but Kay took her time and soon began to catch the stake more often than she missed, missing by smaller and smaller margins. Liza stopped playing—she never came anywhere near the stake, anyway—and concentrated on keeping score, running back and forth with a length of clothesline, and calling out distances. The first time Kay made two ringers in a row, Liza and Mrs. Burger both cheered. "Come on, Dad," said Mr. Burger, handing Burgie his two horseshoes. "You're not going to let her sneak up on you?" Burgie spat tobacco juice, made a ringer, and bounced one.

When Burgie had thirty points, Kay had twenty-five. When Burgie reached forty points, Kay had thirty-seven. Then Kay had a good run, and Burgie had a bad one; both reached forty-six points in the same turn. Everyone else was hopelessly behind. "Come on, Kay!" cried Liza. "Give us a ringer!"

Kay rubbed her grimy hands together and stepped up to the pitch. Liza tried to walk on her hands and fell over as the first horseshoe sailed through the air, clanked against the stake, and fell propped against it.

Mrs. Burger cheered. "Lucky shot!" cried Stu. Burgie stooped with his hands on his knees, like a baseball catcher waiting for the pitch. Liza marched up and down, chanting: "Ringer! Ringer! Ringer!" Kay pushed her hair off her face, frowned, and threw her second shoe. It caught the top of the stake and spun around and down with a metallic clatter. Liza jumped up and down clapping.

"Not bad," said Burgie. Kay made way for him, wordlessly, a smile tugging one side of her face while the other side still frowned in concentration.

"Come on, Granddad!" called Stu, plainly forgetting that he had started out on Kay's side. "Show her what you can do!"

Liza held her breath as the first shoe flew down the pitch to wrap itself noisily around the stake. Stu and Mr. Burger clapped. Kay held her hands tightly in front of her, and Mrs. Burger leaned forward. The second shoe followed the first, precisely—a second ringer.

Kay dropped her hands, and the half-smile vanished. Liza remembered to breathe. Stu and Mr. Burger cheered, and Mrs. Burger relaxed. "Darn! That was close, though!"

Burgie walked over to Kay. "Got to hand it to you! I haven't had to fight that hard for a game in fifteen years."

Kay was silent for an embarrassingly long minute. "Thank you," she said sourly. "I guess I did all right, for a girl."

"Hey, you did swell for anybody," said Burgie, ignoring her tone. Liza squirmed inside. Why did Kay have to be such a poor sport? She was never like this when Mom beat her at checkers. At least Burgie didn't seem to take it personally. He clapped his stomach and turned to Liza. "Got me an appetite! How much longer till dinner, missy?"

Liza looked at her watch and squeaked. One o'clock! The roast'd be burned to a crisp! She dashed into the house, tripping on the doorstep and catching herself before she fell. After the brightness outside, the kitchen was too dark to see, but she knew where she'd left the oven mitts. She had them on her hands and was right on top of the oven before she saw that the roasting pan was already sitting between the burners and the oven was off.

Liza stood still and rubbed her eyes. "Th—good for you, Hobkin!" she whispered, remembering just in time that the fairy encyclopedia said fairies didn't like being thanked. Kay came in. "Is dinner all right?"

"I—I don't know. I haven't looked yet." Clumsy in her oven mits, she peeled back the aluminum foil. The smell rose up in a cloud of steam, making her stomach growl.

Kay peered into it. "Looks like you were just in time. Go wash your hands."

"Your hands are dirtier'n mine."

"So? I'm washing, too. This'll keep a minute or two."

Now that Liza remembered to be hungry, the final preparations for dinner seemed to take forever, even though everyone helped. Stu and Burgie set up the card table and laid out the paper plates, Mrs. Burger made gravy, Kay whipped up peanut butter frosting from the ingredients laid out ready on top of the pantry (which had not been laid out when Liza put the vegetables in), Mr. Burger cut up the roast, and Liza poured milk for everybody and carried the food to the table. Everyone said how good the meal was, except Kay, who was mostly silent. Stu had two helpings of everything and then offered to fetch the desserts.

The Burgers all took pieces of starlight cake with peanut butter frosting and approved it out loud. Not to be outdone in politeness, Liza said, "I'm sure it's nowhere near as good as what you brought," and opened Mrs. Burger's Tupperware. When she saw what kind of cake it was she stared.

"Oh," said Kay.

"What's the matter?" asked Mrs. Burger. "Do y'all not eat German chocolate? I can take it home—it's no problem."

"It's fine," said Kay flatly, in a voice that said plainly it was anything but fine.

Liza couldn't stand that. "It's just right!" she declared. "It's Mom's favorite cake!"

"Was Mom's favorite cake," said Kay sternly, reminding her that Mom was supposed to be dead.

"It's perfect," said Liza, dashing recklessly into the truth. "It's Mom's birthday today. That's why I wanted to do something special. It didn't seem right, ignoring Mom's birthday, but Kay didn't—anyway, I couldn't in a million years have made a good German chocolate cake. Thank you!"

"Oh, honey!" whispered Mrs. Burger, blinking.

Mr. Burger cleared his throat. "I know where your Mom is, she's happy to know you remembered her on her birthday. Fact, I know she'd be pleased and proud of both of you."

Kay scooted back the folding chair and marched into the house without a word. The Burgers looked after her, sympathetically. "She takes things too hard," said Burgie, shaking his head.

"Give her a break, Granddad!" said Stu. "She's doing the best she can. Better than I would."

"She can't keep doing it all alone," said Mrs. Burger.

Suddenly Liza was mad at Kay. She was a poor sport and a liar and bossy, and here these people that she'd never ever been honest to were all worked up about her! "You don't have to feel so sorry for her!" she said. "She's the way she is because she likes it. Nobody made her come out here."

"Of course I don't mean all alone," said Mrs. Burger, obviously misunderstanding her. "She's got you, and that's a lot. But you've got to remember, you've always got her to rely on, and she only has herself." She smiled. "I know you're reliable for your age, but nobody ever really relies on a little sister! Until you get thoroughly grown-up, you always want somebody older."

"Did she ever do anything about finding the

Starks?" asked Burgie. "Some of them must still be around. Willa for one isn't even retirement age yet."

For a minute, Liza considered telling the truth; but Kay would kill her if she did. "She wrote to the schools in Amarillo like you said, Miz Burger, but we never get even junk mail. She says it probably got lost in the bureaucracy."

Mrs. Burger frowned. "I've got a good mind to write them my own self!"

"I don't think Kay would like that," said Liza hurriedly. The open window to Kay's room wasn't three feet away; she was bound to hear. "She thinks we take plenty from y'all already."

"Oh, fiddlesticks! We're just being neighborly." Mrs. Burger picked up a cake cutter she'd brought with the Tupperware. "Who has room for German chocolate in honor of Miz Franklin?"

15

French Fries

It was almost lunchtime, and Liza, alone in the house, craved french fries. At home, Mom had stopped at McDonald's for hamburgers and french fries every payday; but the only time Liza'd had any since running away had been last week when Mrs. Burger took her and Kay into the next town with her and fed them at Dairy Queen. Now her appetite was whetted for grease and salt and light, hot potato.

"It doesn't look that hard," said Liza, studying the directions in the cookbook. The picture showed them cooking in an electric skillet, with a wire basket, neither of which she had; but this did not discourage her. She could heat the oil in a saucepan and fish the fries out with the slotted spatula.

Liza peeled two potatoes in a bowl of cold water on

the gallery, then cut them up, wondering idly why russet potato juice always turned pink when it got out of the potato onto the plate. Today would be long, hot, and boring. Patty and her dad had gone to Abilene to visit her grandparents. Vic was catching up on jobs he should have done last week. The windmill creaked and the locusts buzzed, sounds so common as to be the equal of silence. Liza sang to herself—television commercials, songs she'd learned in school, bits and pieces of rock and country tunes.

The shortening in the saucepan melted but did not look deep enough. Liza added more and waited, nibbling an oatmeal cookie. She had had to sneak out to give Hobkin his share of the cookies last night, because when she tried to set them out with the milk, Kay had scolded her about wasting food. Liza wished Kay wouldn't be such a pig about Hobkin. Sara and Melissa had never had secrets from each other, had never told each other any lies. They had lived in each other's pockets, sharing the same room, the same life in spite of all the years between them; and Sara had known that, no matter what happened or how badly they fought, Melissa would always be on her side against the rest of the world.

It's Kay's fault it's not like that anymore, Liza thought defiantly. She couldn't tell Kay anything about Hobkin; and it was getting easier and easier not to tell her other things, as well. She hadn't mentioned going on the roof after Enid, for instance. She hadn't mentioned the scorpion she'd killed on the woodpile, or the skunky-smelling javelina hogs that had wandered into the mesquite scrub, or daring DeAnn to climb the trellis on Patty's porch. She had had to tell about the dare DeAnn had made her to go into Mr. Fannon's yard with his pit bull and her puppies, because Mrs. Fannon had caught her. If it was going to get back to Kay, anyway, Liza always tried to get her version in first; otherwise, if she knew it would upset her sister, she kept her mouth tight shut.

The melted shortening smoked slightly. The cookbook specifically said not to let it do that, but it didn't say how to stop it. You could tell this cookbook was written by grown-ups. They were always doing things like that—saying don't, or do, and leaving you to figure out how for yourself. That's what's wrong with Kay, thought Liza, dumping in a handful of potato strips. She turned into a grown-up.

The oil roared and frothed, then settled down to bubble quietly. Liza paced the kitchen, chanting one-one thousand, two-one thousand, three-one thousand. She had to make Kay get her a kitchen timer! It was about thirty times as hard to cook if you had to go by your watch—you couldn't relax for a second. No wonder she burned things so often.

Some of the fries floated and some sank. Even the floaters were awkward to catch with the spatula, and drops of hot grease splattered the stove top and her arms as she tried. There had to be a way to do this. If she put the colander on top of a bowl and poured the grease through—ugh, that would get the bowl greasy.

Still, it seemed her best bet. She popped one of the two fries she'd caught into her mouth as she turned to fetch what she needed, and her elbow bumped the handle of the saucepan.

A jet of yellow flame shot up, seemingly halfway to the ceiling. Liza screamed, brain suddenly empty, and found herself at the back door. Grease spat and crackled and stank as it burned, a dark cloud of smoke bulging above the stove. What did you put out grease fires with? She knew, she knew, but she couldn't remember!

The baking soda box flew out of the pantry, across the room, and dumped itself on the blazing stove top. As suddenly as it began, the fire went out, fizzing into thick, choking smoke and a drifting dust of soda. Liza made herself pick up the wet dishrag and walk over to make sure the burners were turned off and all the little bits of flaming grease extinguished before she sat down to start shaking.

"Hobkin? Hobkin, I know you don't like to be thanked, but—" But the whole house could have burned down. She could have started a prairie fire and burned the whole town, or the Burgers' ranch. People and animals could have died, and it would have been all her fault!

By the time Kay got home, Liza had calmed down and cleaned up the kitchen. All her scrubbing could not get the black off the saucepan, nor all the wind that blew, clear the house of the clinging, greasy smell of smoke; and of course, the baking soda was all gone.

Kay sniffed the air and frowned as she put the new bag of ice into the icebox. "You burn something?"

"Yeah," said Liza, trying to sound casual. "We need a new box of baking soda."

"The box we have is practically full—" Kay's tan changed color and she straightened up. Her eyes fastened on Liza's face, and her voice became very low and still. "Liza. What . . . happened?"

"Just a little grease fire," said Liza, looking at her sister's dusty boots instead of at her face. She should have gone for the leather boots. Those JCPenney cheapies weren't standing up to their use. "The baking soda put it right out."

"Grease fire? What were you cooking to make a grease fire?"

"I wanted some french fries, and I thought I could do it. It was dumb. I won't do it again."

"Dumb! Dumb! Dumb doesn't approach what that was! Don't you ever think? You might have knocked that hot grease over and scalded yourself! You might have caught your hair on fire! You might have—you might have—"

"I know what I might have," said Liza. "You don't have to shout. None of that happened, and I know better now. Everything's fine."

"Everything is not fine!" screamed Kay unexpectedly, kicking the corner of the icebox and slamming the door shut so hard it opened again. "We don't have enough money and we're living in a dump without even a toilet for God's sake and I've got to leave you alone all day every day to get up to who knows what—"

"Well, who's fault is that?" Liza shouted back, to her own surprise. She didn't feel angry inside, just blank and shocked and a little scared at the sight of Kay turning red and kicking walls like a kid having a tantrum; but her mouth was opening wide and shouting and her hands were turning into fists. "It was your stupid idea to run off on our own! I was fine! We had you and Mom and Lee all making money and we had TV and air-conditioning and french fries once a week and you had to get up and walk away from it all! Not me, you! And I'm doing the best I can and all you ever tell me anymore is don't do this and we don't have enough money for that and I'm doing the best I can! If that's not good enough maybe we should just go home!"

Kay began to cry. She sat down on the floor as if her legs had given out and shook all over and began to cry. Liza had never seen her do that before—not as Kay, not as Melissa, not as far back as she could remember. It made her sister's face twisted, ugly, and young, all the grown-upness wrung out of it.

Not knowing what else to do, Liza began to cry also and sat down beside her. They hugged each other and rocked back and forth, crying till they were weak. Liza crawled into Kay's room for the Kleenex box, and they blew their noses and cleaned their faces together. At last Kay had her face shoved back into order, and said in a fragile voice, "I'm sorry, Liza. I shouldn't break down in front of you."

"That's okay," said Liza. "I'm sorry I yelled at you."

"Hey, I yelled first." She sniffed again but began to sound more like herself. "And—you were right, up to a point."

"Up to what point?" asked Liza.

"We can't go back. Whatever goes on here, however bad off we get. And we're not so bad off, really. We could be living in a cardboard box in Los Angeles. Only it gets to me sometimes."

"Why can't we go back?" asked Liza. "You don't really think Mom wouldn't take us?"

"No. No, I'm sure she would." Kay looked Liza in the face for a long time as if this would help her find out something, then shook her head and let her shoulders sag. "It's not something I can tell you yet."

"Why not?"

"I just—I can't. When you're bigger. You'll just have to trust me. You trust me, don't you?"

"Of course I do." But this trust was not as simple and obvious as it would have been in May. "Is it a secret?"

"You could call it that. But only because—it isn't because I don't trust you. Never think that. All we've got in the world is each other, and if we don't have that, we don't have anything. You're not old enough to understand."

"I'm a lot older than I was this spring. Try me."

Kay turned her head away, blinking. "I can't. Really. I don't want to talk about it." She cleared her throat. "The principal was in buying Cokes today. He wanted to know about your school transcripts. It's dumb, but I never even thought of that before. We'll have to come up with some good reason not to have them."

Afraid Kay would begin to cry again, Liza let the subject change; but she did not forget.

16

Discoveries

_____ *For a while after the french fry fire*, Kay was more relaxed and talkative, more like Melissa than she had been since she caught Lee tickling Sara. She and Liza played checkers and horseshoes in the evening and talked about things that went on.

Kay worried a lot about winter. "It's hard to believe now," she said, wiping the sweat off her Big Red can, "but it'll get cold. Come December, we might have a day as hot as this, and suddenly a norther will come through, and in ten minutes there'll be ice on the trough. Clovis says there's nothing between here and the North Pole but a bobwire fence."

"We can close off the parlor," suggested Liza, remembering how Aunt Enid had dealt with winter weather in the diary. "We never use it, anyway. And if that's still too much to heat, we can close up my room, too, and live in your room and the kitchen." Liza's checker landed on Kay's last row, so she said, "King me."

Kay topped Liza's checker with a captured piece. "That's true. But we'll still need to fix that place in the roof where it's rusted out. And the more I think about it, the surer I am that we can't do without water in the house this winter, which means getting somebody to lay pipe and buying a new water heater."

"Really? Oh, boy! Can we have electricity, too?"

"No. Mr. Guerra says camping equipment's bound to go on sale in the next couple of months, and I'll get us a Coleman lantern for you to do homework by, if they even let you in school without transcripts."

Liza had been giving some thought to this problem herself. "Patty knows a lot about the way schools are run," she said cautiously, watching Kay's checker slide forward. "And she can keep a secret real good."

"Real well," corrected Kay, "and you're not going to explain the problem to her. We don't need outside help."

"I think we do," said Liza, looking at the board. "And everybody wants to help us. They like us."

"How long do you think they'll keep liking us if they find out we've been lying to them all summer?"

Liza looked up in the middle of her move, surprised that this had even occurred to Kay. "Patty wouldn't tell."

"Not on purpose. But what if she has to get information out of her dad? He might trick the secret out of her." Kay shook her head. "Three can keep a secret if two of them are dead. Don't worry, I'll think of something."

Liza made a list of things around the house that needed fixing. Despite all of Hobkin's care, the list was long. In addition to the rusty place on the roof, which would let water down into the kitchen if it ever rained (and the old men all said, hopefully, that it would likely rain in October), some of the windows had cracked panes, the water heater was rusted out and useless, and some of the floorboards and gallery poles were loose or rotting. The goats would need a winter shelter (Kay refused even to consider giving over Liza's room to them when it got cold) and a larger supply of hay than they now required. Both girls would need winter clothes.

One evening after milking they sat on the back step in the dusk and strained their eyes over pages full of arithmetic as Kay showed Liza how little their dollars in the bank amounted to compared to the cost of all the things they needed. The money Kay made at the store kept them alive from day to day but allowed little over for saving, or even going to movies or buying comic books once in a while. "And we need our savings," Kay said. "What if one of us gets sick or hurt? Besides, this was supposed to be a college fund."

"I don't have to go to college," said Liza.

"I'd like you to at least have the option."

Liza thought hard. There weren't many ways for a

kid her age to make money in a town where one sixth-grade boy could handle all the paper routes. "Maybe I could sell goat's milk."

"You have to be government inspected."

"I could barter it." Barter was like swapping. Mr. Maguire had a book on barter, which said money was too complicated and unfair, and everybody should switch to trading each other goods and services. She hadn't read it, but she'd looked at the description on the book jacket and gotten an idea how the system was supposed to work. "Mr. Maguire knows how to fix roofs and things. Maybe we can get him to do some of the work if we give him some of our milk."

"I doubt we'd have enough. Not the way Enid's drying up." Kay brightened. "You can sell their wool, though. When does your goat book say to shear them?"

Liza let the goat's milk idea drop but did not give it up. She hadn't worried about Enid's milk before, since between them she and Mavis produced as much as she, Kay, and Hobkin could drink; but the next day she studied the goat book for ways of increasing milk production. She discovered something that she had read about before and forgotten. For goats to keep giving milk, they had to be kept "in kid," which meant you had to let them have baby goats.

The book assumed that its readers knew a lot more about goats and the process of getting babies than Liza did. She looked through some of her other books and Aunt Enid's diaries hoping for hints but found none. Grown-up stupidity again! When she grew up and wrote handbooks, she wouldn't assume that anybody reading them knew anything. She'd pretend she was explaining to a Martian and go through every little step. People could just skip what they already knew.

Stu stopped by on his way back from fetching the Burgers' mail, as she was bringing the goats in that evening, and helped her coax them through the gate, leaving his Jeep in the road. "You looking forward to school?" he asked, as they herded Mavis and Enid before them up the drive.

"Nobody looks forward to school," said Liza. She had been to see the school building, an ugly cinderblock stack on the same side of town as the churches. It seemed impossibly far away and alien from the real life she was living here, and much bigger than should have been necessary to house the children of Britt. This was because the children of three similarly sized towns were all bused into Britt.

"I look forward a lot," said Stu, "but then I get to go to college." He poked his thumb in the air, a gesture that meant "Gig 'em, Aggies." What "Gig 'em" meant Liza didn't know. "School's more fun when you learn what you want to learn instead of what the teacher and the government decide is important."

"What do you want to learn?" asked Liza politely.

"I'm going to be a vet. That's why I'm an Aggie. A and M is the best place to learn to be a vet in the whole country. There are medical schools it's not as hard to get into as the Aggie veterinary school."

Liza skipped as she swung the gate closed on Mavis

and Enid's pen. The goats crowded together at their freshly filled drinking trough, slurping up clean water with long tongues. "You know a lot about ranch animals already, don't you?" she asked. "All about cattle and sheep and goats and things?"

"I'm used to dealing with everyday things. Something wrong with your goats?"

They sat on the back step with their ankles in the grass (getting long again, but slowly) and she explained about the milk and needing Enid to get pregnant. "I know there's something awful about getting pregnant," she said apologetically.

"Oh, not really," said Stu easily. "Goats don't embarrass, you know." He proceeded to explain, and it didn't sound awful. The only troublesome part was the stud fees. Since she didn't have a male goat, she would have to borrow somebody else's to father the kids, and it was customary to pay. "I bet Vic's dad'll let you borrow one of his if you let him have one of the kids," suggested Stu. "Goats almost always have twins. You can't keep all of them, anyway. The herd'd get too big too fast."

Mavis and Enid ran to the side of their pen, bleating. "Kay's home," said Liza, rising. They went around the house and met her trudging into the yard with her usual bag of groceries.

Stu tried to take the bag from her, but she ignored his outstretched hand. "Evening," she said. "How you doing?"

"Fine," said Stu.

"He's been helping me," said Liza. "I figured out from the goat book why Enid isn't giving as much milk, but I couldn't figure out from it how I was supposed to get her to have kids, that's baby goats, so I asked Stu and he said—"

Kay's face went hard and still, and she set down the grocery bag, slowly, on the crate on the gallery. "You asked Stu?"

So what was wrong now? "He's going to be a vet, you know, and he knows lots about goats and things already. So he thinks Vic's dad'll let us borrow one of his billies for the father if we give him one of the kids instead of a stud fee, and when she goes in heat—"

Kay wasn't looking at her anymore. Her face reddened as she glared at Stu. "You came here to talk to my little sister about heat and stud fees?"

"I came here to help her bring the goats in," answered Stu. "When she found out I was planning to be a vet, she started asking about animal husbandry. She needs to find out if she's going to get anywhere with the goats."

"Not from you." Kay folded her arms tight and stepped between him and Liza. "She can learn that sort of thing perfectly well from a woman."

"Not from you, she can't," said Stu shortly. He was enough taller than Kay that he had to bend his head to meet her eyes. "Are you the one who gave her the idea there was something awful about getting pregnant?"

"You make me sick!" hissed Kay. "Get off this property and don't come back!"

Liza wanted to sink into the ground.

"All right," said Stu, as if he were working hard not to be angry, "but if you're going to live in the country, you have to learn to relax! The facts of life aren't going to hide themselves away just because you're uptight. I'll see you around."

Liza, to her shame, didn't find her voice till he was already gone. "Why do you have to be so rude?" she demanded. "He was only trying to help me out."

"Maybe," said Kay. "And maybe not. If he'd really wanted to be helpful, he should have told you to ask his mother." She picked up the groceries and stalked into the house.

"Miz Burger wasn't here," objected Liza, following her and helping unload the groceries—hamburger, sour cream, tortillas, and other necessities for tacos. "I don't see what difference it makes who tells me, as long as I find out."

"There's good and bad ways to find things out, and good and bad people to find things out from." Kay slammed a can of refried beans onto the table crate.

"Stu's not bad. He's never been anything but nice to us, and you're always mean to him."

"I am not."

"Well—you're never nice to him." A thought struck her. "Or Vic. You're never nice to any boys at all, except Mr. Guerra, and that's because he's your boss.

Even back home, you were the only girl in the whole twelfth grade that never went on a date."

"What business is that of yours?"

"I know what it is!" said Liza, banging the door of the icebox. "You're a bigot!" She turned to see what effect this terrible word would have on her sister, but all she could see was Kay's back. "You're prejudiced against boys. You're just like one of those nasty people who think people who are a different color, or a different religion, are all bad."

Kay was silent for a long time. "Did you ever think," she said to the sink, "that some prejudiced people might have good reasons for being prejudiced?"

"Don't be dumb. There can't be any good reasons."

"Oh, yes, there can." She got a bowl, filled it from the bucket of water by the back door, and began chopping onion, rinsing the knife blade every time the fumes from the juice threatened to make her cry. "What if a black person or a Mexican, for instance, had done something terrible to someone? But, except when this person was doing terrible things, he looked like anybody else. Looked nice, even." The knife cut through the layers of onion with a clean, soft sound. "The person he'd done it to would go around wondering, is it the same way with every other black person or Mexican? You can't go by how people look. You can't even go by how they act. The really evil people will wait. It's more fun for them if you like them before they hurt you. If they can con you into thinking it's your fault." She rubbed her nose with the back of her hand and rinsed the knife blade.

Liza was not sure she wanted to hear this. "So does that mean you go around not liking anybody ever again? That's dumb."

"I didn't say that," said Kay. Despite rinsing the knife, her voice was clogged and sniffly. "But you have to be careful. There isn't any way to tell, and so—you have to be careful. All the time."

Liza made herself walk up behind Kay and hug her around the waist. "Kay? Who are you talking about?"

"Nobody!" snapped Kay. "I'm just giving an example! Now let go! I can't chop onions straight with you hanging onto me."

"They'll taste the same crooked," said Liza. But she let go and retreated across the room.

Melissa was crying somewhere, and Sara, wandering the hallways of Lee's house, could not find her way back to the room. The house had changed while they were gone—the hallways had stretched, the windows were boarded up. Every time she flipped a light switch, it clicked emptily. The only light came from the kitchen, where Hobkin washed dishes and Mom worked math problems.

Hobkin was so small he had to stand on the kitchen stool to reach the sink, and the sleeves of his ragged shirt dragged in the water. "I can't find Kay," said Liza.

"Kay doesn't live here," said Mom. "I've got to pay the plumber." All the math problems were dollars and cents, like the list Liza and Kay had made, but thousands of dollars for food, and feeding the goats, and buying beer for Lee.

Liza started scratching through things with a Magic Marker. "We don't need beer or TV or electricity," she explained. Mom sighed and stuck her hands in her hair. Mom always made a point of having big hair, to impress the customers in the beauty store; but now she had it cut off short like Aunt Enid's. "Sometimes you just have to live with ticks," said Mom.

Melissa was still crying somewhere—no, it had to be Kay because Melissa never cried. Hobkin hopped off the kitchen stool and skipped down the dark hall, singing, "Grow the wood to rock the bairn to grow the man to lay me!" Liza followed him, running.

"It's not Kay!" called Mom. "It's just Enid and Mavis."

But it wasn't, because the sound came from behind the door of her room; and Kay had been firm about not letting the goats into the house for the winter. Liza pounded on the door, shouting, "Kaylissa! Let me in!" But Melissa couldn't hear her over the TV football game. Liza knew it was a football game even though the announcer was talking too loud to understand.

Suddenly Liza was terrified. Someone was hurting Melissa in there; and if she got in, he'd hurt Sara, too! Liza stopped pounding on the door and backed up, planning to run. "Chicken!" jeered Hobkin from the top of the closed door. She tried to bend her neck back far enough to see how he fitted there. "She didn't leave *you* to him."

Liza jumped up and grabbed his hand. Hobkin hauled her over the door and she fell down the other side. Now I'll wake up, thought a small part of her with relief; but she didn't wake up. She landed on top of the woodpile, and baseball bats scattered as she scrambled down. Lee got up off Melissa and reached for her, his arms growing long to reach across the room. Melissa lay in the crib, naked, repeating over and over and over, "I don't want to talk about it."

Liza fumbled for a baseball bat. Lee smiled at her, his most friendly smile. "Can't you take a joke, Sara?" he asked.

"I'm not Sara! I'm Liza!" screamed Liza, striking out with the bat, and missing wildly. "Hobkin! Bring the Indians! Hobkin!" Where was Kay? Kay should have saved Melissa. Couldn't Mom hear this? "Mom!" screamed Liza, missing and missing and missing as she swung the bat. "Mom! Kay! Kaay!"

Liza sat up. Her dark, familiar room in the rear of the Stark house was still except for the distant sneeze of the owl, and the pounding of blood in her ears. Her whole body felt wet and slick and cold. "Kay?" she whispered, and realized that her mouth was too dry to make a sound.

Shakily she padded barefoot to the door connecting her room to her sister's. Kay was a dark lump in the middle of the moonlit floor, breathing deeply. Evenly.

Liza wrapped herself in her sleeping bag and sat on the step between the rooms, watching her big sister sleep.

17

Willa

——————— *Liza had breakfast ready when Kay* got up: puffed wheat with overripe bananas cut up in it, and Hobkin's coffee. They ate on the gallery, with the breeze cool on their faces. The sun had been up less than an hour, but the grass was dry, and the horny toads chased ants in the sunshine. "I had a bad dream last night," said Liza.

"I'm sorry," said Kay, drinking the milk left in the bottom of her bowl. "What about?"

"We were back home, and you were crying so I broke into our room. Remember the crib I slept in till I was almost in kindergarten? You were in that, and Lee was on top of you."

Kay turned her face away. "It was only a dream. Don't think about it."

"I remember when you got the lock for our door. It wasn't long before we got rid of the crib. You saved up your allowance for weeks and went to the hardware store and got the lock, and screws, and a screwdriver. You had all kinds of trouble putting it on, but you wouldn't ask anybody for help." Liza put down her bowl and leaned against her sister's legs. "Why did you want a lock so bad?"

"I needed my privacy."

"But you weren't private. I was locked in with you."

"Locked in with you was more private than when Mom and Lee could come in any time they felt like it. You know Lee never would knock." For a minute she looked as if she were going to say something else; but all she did was get up to rinse her bowl.

Liza kept busy all that day so she wouldn't have to think about what she suddenly knew, what Kay had been keeping from her. She brushed the goats vigorously before taking them to pasture. She washed all the dirty clothes and hung them to dry. She swept and dusted and spread pesticide over the whole house, made banana bread out of the last of the bananas, and climbed the windmill just to prove she could. When Patty came over, they had a picnic in the graveyard, where Liza was inspired to tear up all the weeds around Larry's grave. In the process they caught a six-inch hognose snake, which they confined in Patty's lunchbasket while discussing what to do with it.

When their hands were sore from pulling weeds, they rode back into town, found Leti playing the videogame at the Rock Hard Café, and dropped the snake down the back of her oversized T-shirt. Her reaction was so much more violent than expected (who could be afraid of a hognose snake?) that they beat a hasty retreat and spent the rest of the afternoon with an eye toward avoiding her vengeance. They didn't see her again, but DeAnn and two or three lesser girls always showed up if they hung around in one place too long. They played with Patty's kitten, got ice cream (which Patty paid for) from the drugstore, and helped Mr. Maguire lay carpet in Patty's room. In the evening, Mr. Maguire discovered he had no bread for supper and offered to take Liza as far as the store. Not once did she mention her dream or the secret Kay had kept for so long.

At the store, Kay was wiping the counter and Mr. Guerra was fiddling with the cash register—it was an old one and the drawer kept jamming. At the counter, Clovis drank a cup of coffee around a lipful of snuff and read last week's county paper. "Hi, young lady," he said cheerfully. "I hear you been painting the town red."

Kay stopped wiping the counter and fixed Liza with a stern face. "What's this we hear about you scaring Leti half to death with a snake?"

How had she found that out already? "It was only a hognose," said Liza. "And she deserved it."

"She didn't deserve to be made so hysterical Dr. Foster had to give her a sedative!"

"A sedative?" said Mr. Maguire, pausing between

wheat and white bread. "I would have said Leti had nerves of steel. Last winter she did a tightwire act on the top of the swings that nearly gave me a heart attack."

"She's only like that about snakes," explained Mr. Guerra. "When she was tiny she was bitten by a rattlesnake, and it almost killed her. I'm surprised Vic never told you about that, Liza. Luckily her big brother knew the right first aid and kept her going till they got her to the county hospital; but she's got a genuine phobia about snakes now."

"That's right," said Clovis, nodding sagely. "Those shocks you get when you're young, you never get over them. I've seen that little girl stop dead in a sweat while a baby grass snake wiggled across the sidewalk."

Liza felt cold and sick. "I didn't mean to scare her that bad. I didn't know."

"Well, you'll have to march into town and apologize bright and early tomorrow," declared Kay, "and I don't ever want to hear anything about you playing practical jokes anymore."

Mr. Maguire didn't say anything, but from the look on his face Liza knew Patty would get a talking-to when he got home. She did not bother to explain about the horny toads someone had put in Patty's cot on the porch one evening last week or DeAnn and Leti's general rudeness. "If you let me have the meat, I'll go home and start dinner," she offered humbly.

"I haven't gone to the co-op," said Kay. "There's a bus coming in tonight, so I'll have to stay late and eat supper here. Can you manage with a Frito pie or something? Or you want to hang around here till I go home?"

"I've got to bring the goats in," said Liza.

She stopped to look at the comic book rack on her way out. Mr. Guerra had finally gotten in some of the ones she had read right before they ran away. Next month he would get new ones, but she wouldn't be able to buy any. She wouldn't even ask Kay if she could have money for some.

As she crossed the highway, a dusty, dark green car turned at the twin mailboxes. She wondered who was visiting the Burgers.

Mavis and Enid were in a contrary mood. They danced, and bleated, and charged imaginary enemies. Liza was almost glad. Goat naughtiness was one more thing to distract her from the terrible things she knew now and had not known yesterday. The goats were so much trouble that she didn't see the dusty dark green car in the yard till Enid and Mavis ran away from her to sniff it.

Liza was so surprised she didn't feel nervous till she had already called out, "Who's there?" Then she thought of all the people it might be—a maniac going around the country slicing up little girls, a detective hired to track runaways down and take them home, even Lee, who was always trading off his old cars for new ones, so her not recognizing this one wouldn't mean anything. She had a moment of blind fear, and then an old woman came around from the back.

She had hair the color of Mavis's wool and was not much taller than Liza, but her back was yardstick straight. Freckles speckled her dry, loose skin. She wore a flowered dress, like most old women in Britt, and bore the familiar dried-up lines on her face, but Liza had never seen her before. "Hello," she said. "Which of the Franklin girls are you?"

"Liza," said Liza. "Kay's working late at the store."

"I see." Enid stopped sniffing the car and ran up to the old lady. Instead of flinching, the woman reached out her hand gently for the goat to sniff, then scratched her poll. "I'm pleased to meet you. My name is Willa Stark."

"Oh," said Liza, and couldn't think of anything else to say.

Willa helped her pen the goats. "I'm impressed with the way you've kept the place," she said conversationally. "It's a big job for two girls all on their own."

"Kay's a grown-up now," said Liza defensively, though there was no hint of accusation or blame in Willa Stark's manner. "And people are helpful. And there's Hobkin." She watched Willa's face to see how she took this last remark.

"He's still here?" asked Willa in surprise. "We thought he must have gone back to England when Mama died."

"No, he stayed and kept the place nice for you. Kay doesn't believe in him."

"Poor Hobkin!" said Willa. "Daddy never believed in him, either. And all us children went through a stage—a long stage—when we were too embarrassed to believe."

Liza felt awkward, and relieved. "Well. Come in this house"—using the hospitable, West Texas phrase hesitantly—"and have something to drink."

She couldn't tell what the house's rightful owner thought of the soda crates, the cleaning supplies lined up by the back door, the rinsed and crushed aluminum cans collecting in the empty parlor awaiting Mr. Guerra's annual trip to the recycling center. Even with the front and back doors and all the windows open, the kitchen was dim and hot, and she didn't like to ask such an old lady to sit on the floor, so they took their cans of root beer onto the gallery, and Willa—Miss Stark, she couldn't call an old lady by her first name!—sat on the soda crate. Liza was tired down to her bones. "We've been letting folks think we were your long-lost nieces," she blurted out, "but we're not."

"I know," said Miss Stark. "I know who and where all my nieces and nephews are. But don't worry. I didn't tell Jonna Burger that."

"When did you talk to Miz Burger?"

"Last night. She wrote to my school district trying to find me. I assumed it was about the property. When I called her, she told me all she knew about y'all, and I told her not to mention anything to you until I'd had a chance to look over the lie of the land." She drank her soda, gazing at the mesquite tops. "Who are you, really, Liza Franklin?"

Liza leaned her head against the doorsill. In the

heat, her whole body was one huge pulse, with which the creaking windmill turned in rhythm. Her head and the back of one ear ached. "Sara Welch," she said, "and Kay's real name is Melissa. We ran away."

Miss Stark sipped root beer, watching the darkness creep from east to west, reflecting patches of the sunset that blazed, unseen, behind the house. Whenever Liza stopped talking, Miss Stark asked a question—just one, just the right one. The story was hopelessly mangled, all the least important parts told first because the important parts were new and hard to tell.

"I think I must have seen Lee hurting Melissa. When I was real little, before they got rid of the crib. Only I was still little enough to forget it. You think that's why she got the lock? So I wouldn't see what went on?"

"It wouldn't surprise me," said Miss Stark.

"You think—you think the lock stopped him?"

"I doubt it. That sort of man isn't stopped by a lock."

"Then why didn't she say something?" Liza was having trouble with her voice. It wanted to shout, and whisper, and howl, and choke, all at the same time. "Why didn't she do something before? She didn't have to wait till she thought he was going to hurt me to run away. She could have—she could have gotten the baseball bat before then. She could have told Mom."

"It's possible she did," said Miss Stark, "or she may have had a reason not to. Maybe not a good reason. Remember she was scared, and confused, and he would have done everything he could to keep her quiet.

You don't know what lies he told her or what threats he made."

"She never seemed scared. Only . . . funny about men."

"She wouldn't want to seem scared in front of you. It looks to me as if her main concern was always protecting you."

"It shouldn't have been! She should've protected herself!"

"Yes. But it's hard to know what's best to do all the time."

Liza hugged her knees and stared at the ground. The bare dirt was seamed with cracks, making crisp little polygons that looked as if they could be lifted out whole, like cookies. "So what'll happen to us now? You won't make us go back, will you?"

"You're not hurting the house. We've got lots of time to decide things in."

The east was navy blue now, and the stars were coming out. Liza's stomach growled. "Would you like some supper?"

"Yes, please. When do you milk the goats?"

"Cripes!" Liza jumped up. "I forgot all about it! Why aren't they bleating?"

The reason was clear when they hurried through the house and found the milk bucket already standing, covered, by the door. The clothes were there, too, clean and folded in the laundry basket.

"Good old Hobkin!" said Miss Stark. "Land, but I'm sorry I treated him so bad! But when the whole

world around you thinks fairies are for tiny children—
well, I'm not the first person to snub an old friend
from embarrassment. I know better now."

Miss Stark lit the new Coleman lamp while Liza
strained the milk. "Why did he come here with Aunt
Enid?" Liza asked.

"Oh, he'd been in her family forever. But Mama
was the last of her family in England. When she was a
nurse in the war—World War I, you know—she still
had a grandmother; but late in the war came a flu
epidemic and it hit Mama's hometown bad. She buried
her grandma and married Daddy on the same day,
and Hobkin followed her out to Texas."

"People don't die of the flu," objected Liza.

"They did in 1918. Millions of them. Seems like half
the graves in that old graveyard down the road are for
flu victims. So Mama and Hobkin came to Texas. I was
grown up before I realized how brave that was." She
carried the lamp to the pantry crate and examined the
available cans. "I was born here and never thought
there was any other place to live than Texas. Still
don't. But Mama barely spoke the same language as
the folks around here. The work was enough to break
her all by itself, and then the heat was something awful.
Her part of England was cold, and wet. Here it'll go
six or seven years without raining. She'd get up in the
morning, look at the sky like she couldn't believe it
was still there. She might as well have been on a different planet. I don't think she would've managed without
Hobkin. He was all she had left of home."

"Why'd she come here, then?" asked Liza.

"I asked her that, once. When I came back from teacher's college in Austin, I had a faint idea how homesick she must be, because Austin was about as strange and scary as I could take. And what she said was, she had a choice between a hard life in Texas with my daddy and a hard life in England without him."

Liza relaxed as they cooked and ate a dinner of vegetable soup and corned beef hash. Miss Stark talked about her brothers and sisters, and Hobkin, and her mother and father. Liza had never thought about Rankin Stark before—Aunt Enid had seemed more important—but the way Miss Stark talked about him, he grew to equal his wife. She told a funny story about how he tried to help with the housework when Aunt Enid was sick and did a bad job because men in those days didn't know anything about housework. Hobkin had to help him, and—because he didn't believe in Hobkin—Mr. Stark had to invent explanations for the floor being swept clean, the baby fed, and the water coming in without him. Willa and her brothers and sisters got more credit than they deserved that time.

It was dark and they were laughing together as they washed the dishes, when Enid and Mavis started the raucous bleating that always preceded an arrival. "There's Kay," said Liza, drying her hands. Suddenly she felt like a stretched rubber band again. "She's going to kill me when she finds out what all I told you. Let me go meet her alone first, okay?"

She ran into the yard. Coming out from the brightness of the Coleman lamp, and with the moon almost
wasted away in the sky, it was hard to see—the mesquites a mass of black against the star-dotted sky, the
car a looming shadow. "Kay?" she called. "You're
awful late."

"I know." Her voice sounded strained. "There's
a—there's a surprise here for you."

A surprise? Liza walked around the car, blinking
and staring into the dark. Kay was a shadow coming
up the drive beside a taller shadow. Liza noticed a new
smell in the air, alien to the West Texas night. A smell
like hairspray and beauty parlors. And the shadow
wasn't really much taller than Kay, it just looked that
way because of the big hair—

"Mom!" she shouted, and ran to her.

18

Mom

———————— *By the moth-flickered light of the* Coleman lantern, Mom's face was as pale as the owl's, except for the bruise running from her cheek down to her neck. Liza couldn't look away from that bruise. Mom had gotten it when Lee found the furnished apartment she'd moved to after Kay and Liza ran away and had shoved her face into a door frame. Always when the girls were around, Mom explained calmly, he had hit her where the bruises would be covered by her clothes. Being left alone had upset him so that he didn't care anymore whether they showed or not.

"But why didn't you do something?" demanded Liza. Willa Stark had left them to themselves, and they were all in the back room, sitting on an opened sleeping bag. "You could have hit him back, or called the police, or—or something."

"He only did it once in a while," said Mom, as if she were talking about him staying out late or hogging the bathroom. "I never could have won a fight with him. He was too much stronger than me. And I needed him. Even with his paycheck, we had a hard time making ends meet. I was sure we couldn't manage without it. But"—she turned to Kay, and her eyes were like two more bruises in her face—"if I'd known what he was doing to you, I never would have stayed a day, if I'd known he was hurting you, too. Why didn't you tell me?"

"What would you have done if I had?" asked Kay. She sat at the extreme edge of the light, where her face did not show, and her voice was bitter and impatient. "When I was Liza's age he told me you wouldn't believe me and if I told he'd—well, never mind. I was too scared of him to tell anybody. And you jumped every time he said frog. I thought you were crazy in love with him."

"I was, once." Mom looked at her hands folded in the hollow of her crossed legs.

Liza was tired and cross. She had never been up this late in her life before, she hadn't gotten much sleep the previous night, and the whole world was changing under her feet. Mom and Kay had been saying approximately the same things to each other since Miss Stark left. "What difference does it make?" she asked, sprawling on the sleeping bag between them. "Everybody kept secrets but me. Or, anyway, I didn't till Kay made me. But it's all gone now. We don't have to mess with Lee. Everything'll be fine."

Mom sighed and fingered her bruise.

"I wish it were that easy," said Kay. "Lee liked having us to pick on. He's not going to sit quietly and let us get away."

"So what? He doesn't know where we are."

"He knows where I work," said Mom. "That's how he found me. They gave me time off to look for y'all, but I have to go back Monday, and I don't have a plan. Since Mary Alice's mother showed me that letter, I've been moving heaven and earth to find you, but I never once thought what to do when I did."

"Great, Mom. That's always the problem, isn't it? You don't think ahead!"

Mom's face twisted and her eyes blinked. Liza turned on Kay. "Oh, shut up! I think she was smart to find us. The postmark doesn't even say Britt! All she knew was which big town we were closest to, and we're not all that close to it. Aren't you glad to see her?"

"I guess so," grumped Kay, "but she keeps messing things up. We would all have been fine if she hadn't married Lee. And us two were doing okay till she came along. She came right up to me in the store and called me by name! By now the whole town knows we're liars."

"Miss Stark would've told everybody anyhow," Liza pointed out.

Kay put her head on her knees and groaned. "Oh, everything's falling apart!"

"I know," said Mom, "but we'll have to do the best we can. Now I've got y'all back again I'm not afraid of anything. Not really. When we go back to San Antonio I'll—"

"I'm not going back to San Antonio," said Kay flatly. "I won't set foot in the same town as Lee ever again."

"But darling, we have to. My job's there."

"So go back to your job and let us tough it out on our own."

They stared at each other over Liza's head. Liza was fed up. "What do you need that job for, anyway?" she asked. "There's beauty stores in Midland and San Angelo and places like that. Heck, there's one in Britt nobody's using. I bet you could rent it cheap and everybody in Britt'd be glad not to have to drive forever to get their hair done."

"Oh, but I couldn't—"

"How do you know?" Liza tried to roll herself up in a corner of the sleeping bag. "I never thought I could live so long without TV and electricity and a bathroom, for crying out loud, but I'm fine." Something Miss Stark had said earlier—much earlier, what seemed like years and years before this endless night—bobbed into her head. "You've only got two choices. You can have a hard life with Lee or you can have a hard life without him. I know which I'd pick!"

An unfortunately-timed yawn lessened the force of this speech, but she saw Mom's face go still and quiet as she leaned forward and slid her arms around Liza. "Poor Sara," she said, her voice so soft and familiar it made Liza's face hurt. "We've kept you up way too late, arguing about things you shouldn't have to even know about."

"My name's not Sara anymore," objected Liza, "and I'm sick to death of not knowing things!"

They tucked her up in the sleeping bag and carried the Coleman toward Kay's room, still talking softly but audibly. It seemed to bother Mom that the girls had taken new names. "It's got nothing to do with the names as names," Kay told her. "Watch it—remember there's a step down here. Melissa was a victim. I won't be her anymore, that's all. And Sara never did a stroke of work, but Liza—"

Liza sat straight up, tangling in the sleeping bag as she tried to stand. Mom paused in the doorway. "Honey? What's wrong?"

"I forgot to feed Hobkin!" said Liza, forgetting that Hobkin was one of the many things Mom hadn't heard about yet.

"Liza, go back to bed!" said Kay sharply. "Those skunks can do without their milk for one night."

"Skunks?" said Mom nervously.

"Hobkin's not a skunk!" Liza shoved between them into her sister's room. "I'm not going to let you make me tell any more lies, whether you believe me or not. He's a brownie and he works hard and he deserves his milk. He's the one that put out the grease fire, not me, and he did the milking and brought in the clothes tonight and I think he got you your job, so you just lay off!"

"Grease fire?" said Mom.

Kay took hold of Liza's shoulders firmly but not roughly. "Liza. You're talking garbage. Go back to bed. Now."

"You can't make me," said Liza.

Kay's fingers tightened on her angrily, then let go. "All right. Fine. I'll put Hobkin's milk out for him, and we'll discuss it in the morning. Okay?"

Liza searched her face for a lie and found none. "Okay."

She stumbled back to bed but did not sleep till she heard the back door open and shut. The sound of her mother and big sister talking, talking, talking blended with the familiar creaks, rustles, and calls of the summer night.

They talked for three days.

A lot of it was grown-up talk, running around to judges, builders, the lady who owned the beauty store, the bank. Miss Stark stayed at the Desert Breeze Motel and made phone calls to her living brothers and sisters, for they all owned the property equally. The first day was Sunday, and they did not have dinner at the Burgers'; the second day was Monday, and Mom called her boss on the pay phone in the Rock Hard Café, telling her she wasn't coming back and to send her last paycheck to general delivery in the city that processed the area mail. She told her boss three times not to let anyone know where the check had gone.

After a certain point, very little of this concerned Liza. Her name was going to legally be Liza Franklin, and Mom and Kay were going to make sure none of them had to worry about Lee anymore. Whether or not they stayed in Britt depended on a lot of things Liza had no control over, so she went on with the important things—preparing for Enid to be bred to one of the Guerra billies, apologizing to and making a truce with Leti, and controlling Vic's version of the real story behind her and Kay.

"So what's your real names?" he asked on Tuesday afternoon.

"That's none of your business," declared Liza. She and Patty and Vic sat in a row on the graveyard wall, eating sandwiches made from Sunday leftovers and watching Enid, Mavis, and Jughead trim the grass and weeds around the stones. Every time Enid or Mavis showed an inclination to climb out and study the edges of the highway, one or the other of them hopped up and prevented her.

"But what was your stepdad doing to you?" asked Patty.

"He didn't do anything to me," said Liza. "Kay and Mom won't give me the gory details of what he did to them, and, anyway, that's not anybody's business, either."

"You saw the bruise on her mom's face," said Vic. "That's enough for anybody! I bet he was a raging maniac."

"Mom wouldn't have married him if he had been. He looked ordinary and he acted ordinary when he wasn't hurting people. That's how Mom and Kay hung on so long. It'd still be going on if Kay hadn't been afraid he'd start hurting me, soon, and planned how to run away."

"Wasn't it hard?" asked Vic. "I mean, she had to have a social security number and everything from the government."

"It's easy getting fake ID," said Patty wisely. "High school kids in Houston get them all the time for getting into night clubs and things."

"Yeah, but they don't use them to get jobs with."

"She got the idea off a TV show, and then she found a book about it," said Liza vaguely.

"But isn't it illegal?"

"Sort of. But Kay's too young to go to jail." She hoped. "And we all have to stay Franklins, so Lee doesn't find us again."

"And you're staying in Britt, right?" Patty asked anxiously.

"If we can. Miss Stark wants to buy the house off her brothers and sisters so she can retire in it after she quits teaching, and she says it'd be better to have a tenant in it until then than have it stand empty. And Mom may be able to rent the beauty store and run it. She'll have to use my college money to start up on, and

Kay's all upset about that; but I told her I could give up college for her and Mom if I wanted to." She jumped up and ran to clap her hands under Mavis's nose, pushing her down off the wall. "No! Get down, you stupid goat!"

"I'm glad you're staying," said Patty. "I'd die if I had to go through another whole school year with no friends."

"So what am I, chopped liver?" asked Vic.

Patty made a face at him. "You're just a boy. You wouldn't understand."

"I understood better than to put a snake down Leti's back! Cripes, I can't let you two out of my sight!"

"It's not our fault you never told us the one story it was important for us to know," said Liza, gazing over the gravestones at the flat, endless land. She wrapped her hand around a sweating soda can and wiped the cool damp onto her forehead. "I hope we do stay. I don't want to start all over. And I want to move the goat pen and make a garden where it is now. I've been putting fresh bedding down on top of the old stuff like it says in the book, and it's supposed to be great fertilizer."

Vic made a face, tossing the last of his bread crust out for the doves and kicking the wall with his heels. "Yuck! You'll wear yourself out trying to make a garden! You'll have to water it, and hoe it, and pick the bugs out of it, and then everything'll die, anyway, except the thing you like least, and you'll have so much of that you'll be begging to give it away."

"It can't be as bad as that," said Patty. "Anyway, she'll have Hobkin to help her."

"Yeah, I guess I will," said Liza. "I'm telling Mom about Hobkin tonight." She could see the rock where the bonfire had been and, deep in her mind, could hear Hobkin singing, alone among the dancing *nenuhpee*:

"The acorn's not yet fallen from the tree
That's to grow the wood to cradle the bairn
To grow the man to lay me."

19

Laying Hobkin

————————— *Tuesday night Liza and Mom made* dinner for Miss Stark, who brought them an old cable spool in the back of her car to use as a table with the eternal soda crates as chairs. Mom was almost as pleased as Liza to have it—two days of sitting on the floor to eat had been enough for her. "I don't know what we're going to do about furniture," she said anxiously, as they set the spool on end in the middle of the kitchen and admired the effect. "I didn't dare take more away from Lee than I could carry in one trip on the city bus. Most of it's in his name, anyway."

"Don't worry about it!" said Liza. Whenever Mom thought too much about all the things they didn't have, she got panicky. "We don't need all that stuff."

Mom dished up the food while Liza wiped down the table, Kay poured the iced tea, and Miss Stark set out the crates to sit on. "When I think about you kids living all summer without even running water, I feel like I'm going to have to wake up soon," said Mom. "I didn't think y'all could survive without air-conditioning."

"We had more important things to worry about," said Kay.

Miss Stark laughed. "My, it's nice to hear a modern child think there are more important things than air-conditioning!"

"Hobkin was a big help," said Liza, picking up the bowl of broccoli and looking defiantly at Kay.

"Who's Hobkin?" asked Mom.

"An imaginary person," said Kay.

"No," said Miss Stark, "he's the luck of the place."

Mom paused with the plate of ham in her hands and looked around at each speaker in turn. "This isn't helping much," she said. "Sara—I mean, Liza—why don't you tell me about him?"

So Liza told them. Sometimes Miss Stark nodded, sometimes Kay got angry, and all the time Mom ate, made sure the food and drink kept moving, and never spoke. When Liza sang the verse Hobkin had danced to with the *nenuhpee*, Miss Stark frowned slightly, looking over her shoulder out the open back door. When she told how the *nenuhpee* had descended on her and pinched her, Mom made a sound with her throat and Kay changed color under her tan. When she told about the woodpile, and a little later about the grease fire, Mom swallowed and closed her eyes.

"You never told me about Enid getting on the roof," said Kay accusingly.

"It would've just upset you. And there wasn't any point telling you about Hobkin. You know I tried. I never kept any secrets or told any lies if you didn't make me."

Kay started to say something, but Mom stopped her with a lifted hand. "We know you wouldn't on purpose. But you've always been so . . . imaginative, and you've been out here all alone—"

"I'm not crazy, if that's what you mean," said Liza, trying not to feel hurt. "Ask Vic and Patty. Ask Miss Stark."

"I know it's a lot, asking you to believe in fairies," said Miss Stark, sounding like a teacher explaining some wonder of science, "but it's true. I knew him all my life. So did my mother. I've got a stack of her diaries at home, where she talks about him just the same as about her family and the neighbors. I wish I had one here. I'd show you how ordinary he seemed to her."

"Oh," said Liza, scooting back her crate. "Just a minute." She ran to her bedroom, chewing, and fetched Aunt Enid's diaries. "I found these in the parlor under some newspapers," she said, giving them to Miss Stark. "I should've given them to you when you showed up, but I forgot."

Miss Stark's face changed, and she turned the pages as if they were made of glass. "Oh, my! I looked and looked for these after she died and finally decided she hadn't kept a diary for those years." Moving her plate aside, she turned the pages and read bits out loud. " 'Nita croupy. Up half the night and overslept, but Hobkin started breakfast and made coffee.'

" 'Had to scold Hobkin. Cousin Maurine scared Ranny with a javelina hog's head and was out half the night, pixy-led.' "

"Pixy-led?" said Kay.

"You know, like Hobkin did to Randy Phelps," said Liza. "Got him lost."

" 'Gray day. Homesick. Took the babies in my lap and sang the old songs for them; Hobkin rocked the cradle and listened, till I forgot a verse in "Fair Annet," and he sang it out for me. Good to hear a home voice, even invisible!' "

Liza, having read some of this before, cleared the table around people, serving her first attempt at pie as Miss Stark read. The crust was dark and bumpy on top and would have been vastly improved by ice cream.

" 'Heard Ranny screaming, ran in yard to find him and Hobkin killing a rattler,' " read Miss Stark.

"There aren't any rattlers in this yard," objected Kay. "It's not rocky enough."

"It's not any less rocky now than it was then, and Larry was bitten right on the doorstep." Miss Stark closed her eyes and shuddered slightly. "I tell my classes hardly anybody dies of snakebite in a given year, and they eat up rodents, and if you leave them alone they'll leave you alone; but I was four years old and not five feet away when Larry got bit and I'll never, ever, ever feel good around those things!"

"Clovis and Burgie say Hobkin keeps the snakes out since then," said Liza.

"Sounds to me like closing the door after the horse got out," snorted Kay. "I don't think much of a spirit that waits to protect his people from a danger till after it's already struck."

"Hobkin's a brownie, not a god," said Miss Stark. "They didn't have rattlesnakes in England. I reckon it never occurred to him he should keep the snakes out, till Larry died and we all got to hate the sight of one."

"Do you think Hobkin's homesick? Or lonesome?" asked Liza abruptly.

"I don't want to be part of this discussion," said Kay, pushing back her chair. "Excuse me while I milk the goats."

"He shouldn't be lonesome anymore," said Mom. "He's got you and Kay."

"Not to talk to. We're not his kind. We're not even as much his kind as the little Indians."

"What makes you think of that?" asked Miss Stark.

"That song. In the fairy encyclopedia there's a song like it, sung by one who wants to go away. They can't leave till you give them clothes, unless you're mean to them."

"Are you thinking of laying Hobkin?"

"I don't want to! But it isn't fair. He ought to be able to go back to England or live with the little Indians if he wants. But if he'd rather stay with us I don't want to make him go away."

"Why don't you ask him then?" asked Kay crossly, rattling the clean milk pails. "If he's smart enough to sing along with Aunt Enid, he's smart enough to answer a simple question."

"Oh," said Liza, feeling stupid. "I never thought of that."

She tried that night when she left a bowl of milk and a slice of pie out for him. The bats performed their acrobatic feats around the windmill. The owl floated into the starry, moonless sky. Either the javelinas were back or someone had annoyed the skunks, because a faint stink of musk hung on the wind. Mavis licked salt in the pen while Enid arranged herself so as to leave as little space on the bedding for Mavis as possible. Inside, Kay and Mom heated bathwater and argued about money. "Hobkin?" called Liza softly. "Hobkin, do you want me to lay you? Do you want to leave?"

There was no answer, only the lonely, distant howl of coyotes. Underneath the heat of the night on her skin, Liza's flesh felt cold. She went inside.

She and Kay shared a room again, side by side on their sleeping bags, while Mom slept in the front room. Liza had expected to mind, but she didn't. She and Kay had not talked back and forth before going to sleep all summer. "I wish you believed in Hobkin," she said.

"I wish you didn't," said Kay.

"But he's real!"

"Maybe. I don't know anymore. But you can't afford to go around expecting a brownie to take care of you."

"I don't!"

"You got him to cut the grass for you, didn't you? And you never even tried to learn to make coffee. It's like he was a slave or something." Liza, thinking of Vic's plan to put Hobkin to work building a bat tower and cleaning out the barn and of the garden she meant to have next year, said nothing. "Anyway, he doesn't sound safe to me. All that pinching."

"He rescued me from the Indians."

"Not till you were black and blue all over. And look what he did to Nita and Vic, just for being curious."

"He put out the grease fire."

"I'm not saying he's no good. He just makes me nervous."

"I bet he wouldn't if he were a she," said Liza spitefully.

The room was quiet for a long, long time. "Maybe not," said Kay, when Liza was almost too near asleep to understand her. "But I'd rather not have him around."

Finding clothes to fit a brownie is not easy.

Miss Stark helped; but once the school year started, she was not available except on weekends and not always even then. Patty and Vic thought getting rid of

Hobkin was a stupid idea and refused to assist. Liza bought cloth and a pattern with some money Mom let her have for her own and started sewing him a shirt. Sewing was boring; and it was easy to avoid doing it, with all the other stuff that was happening—school, breeding Enid, the plumbing going in, helping Mom make the beauty store functional, Girl Scout meetings, arguing about money and whether or not Mom should call Mary Alice's mother to go collect their stuff from Lee. The plumbing was wonderful, cutting in half the time it took to wash clothes, even without a washing machine; and Liza was sure she'd never grumble about taking a shower again.

School was not as bad as she had expected. The truce after Liza apologized to Leti became permanent, and DeAnn seemed unable to carry on the feud without Leti. Nor did anybody seem to understand that Liza wasn't really a Stark. Everyone seemed to think that the only lie had been about Mom being dead, and though she wasn't sure exactly what people believed about their reasons for that lie, Liza could tell no one held it against her.

One hot September evening, a large package stood by the Franklin mailbox when Liza, Vic, and his big sister Hester got off the school bus.

"Hey, since when do you get mail?" asked Vic.

"We don't," said Liza; but the name on the package was Franklin. The return address was a white label— Mr. and Mrs. George Fraga—and the postmark was

San Antonio. "Oh, wow! Mary Alice's folks must've gotten some of our stuff from Lee!"

Vic had to help her carry the box to the house, so she had to invite him and Hester in to watch her slice it open with her pocketknife. The contents were a hodgepodge of an old life: old clothes, stuffed animals, Sara's jewelry box with its plastic rings and tarnished necklaces, and other shabby, half-forgotten things. The electric skillet and hand mixer would be useful after Miss Stark put in the electricity, but that wouldn't be for a while yet, not till the roof was fixed. Even many of the books were surprisingly uninteresting—Mom's Harlequin romances, Melissa's books about escaping from the Nazi prisons, Sara's comics and mysteries. She was glad to see her issues of the *Power Pack* comic (which Mr. Guerra didn't stock) bagged in plastic and packed flat; but when Vic pounced on the stack and asked to borrow them, she let them go without hesitation.

Two letters were in the bottom of the box—one addressed to Mom from Mrs. Fraga, one to Sara from Mary Alice. After Vic and Hester left, Liza tidied away the packing material and sat on the gallery to read hers. She felt bad that she hadn't thought about Mary Alice in a month.

Dear Sara,

I know that's not your name anymore, but I can't help it. When you ran away I was mad at you for a long time, and after I got over that I found out you weren't ever coming back so I was mad some more but I'm all right now. Have a nice life. My new best friend's name is Margo French. She has red hair and a Siamese cat and can skateboard better than anybody. I hope you make new friends out there wherever you are. Mom knows where because of your mom calling us, but she won't tell me because she thinks Lee might try to find out from me. Don't be mad that your letter gave you away. Mom got at it before I did, or I would have kept it a secret forever. Luckily she knew better than to show it to anybody but your mom. It must be scary living in a haunted house, but I can see where it would be scarier living with Lee. My folks explained about what he was doing to your mom and Melissa. I'm glad you got away before he started on you. Mom and Dad went after your stuff and Lee acted real nice with them, like he couldn't understand why y'all were being so mean, but they didn't pay him any mind. I wish I had a goat, but my mom says no way.

Love,

Mary Alice

Mary Alice's signature had changed. She was making her *M*'s and *A*'s large and curly and the other letters tiny, with a circle over the *i* instead of a dot. Liza sat on the gallery, feeling sad. Mary Alice, her old toys, her old books—none of that was important anymore. She had gone on to other things, whether she wanted to or not; and now she didn't even want to go back.

Liza swept the floor, tidied up her books, animals, and clothes, and took in the wash Mom had hung out that morning. She was not aware of planning it, but by the time she had done all that, she was ready to sit down and finish Hobkin's shirt.

Now that she had finally, truly made up her mind, it wasn't that hard. Miss Stark had found a pair of overalls in a child's size, and even a pair of boots for a toddler that they hoped would fit. Once Liza finished the shirt, Mom showed her how to run up some underwear out of the leftover material. The boys' store in town had a gimme cap that could be adjusted small enough even for a baby. The outfit might not fit, but it was the best Liza could do.

"I can't believe this," said Kay, reverting to disbelief as Liza laid everything on the back step with the milk and a plate of fresh oatmeal cookies. "They'll still be there in the morning, and you will have wasted good money on fairy clothes."

"Leave her alone," said Mom, swishing water in the sink, "and pump up the lamp so she can do her homework."

Mom and Kay argued a lot lately, but mostly Kay gave in, having lost the grown-up edge that kept her silent and bossy. Mom and Melissa had never argued. They had hardly ever talked—afraid, Liza realized now, of letting each other in on their secrets. She arranged her offerings neatly and sat back trying to think of something to say to Hobkin; but she had a whole chapter to do in math, and a test in social studies, and Mom and Kay had started talking about Miss Stark's plan to sell the parlor organ to an antique dealer and use the money for furniture. Liza went inside.

Enid and Mavis, Hobkin and the owl, skunks, javelinas, deer, Vic, Mary Alice—only she was Patty, too—and little Indians were dancing around the bonfire. Bats swooped in and out, catching huge brown moths around the flame. Liza watched them and wanted to cry, but the thudding of the drums in her belly and blood tickled, making her laugh instead. She tried to sing along, but the words escaped her. She tried to catch at the dancers as they whirled by—Enid and Mavis, Aunt Enid and Rankin Stark, cats, bats, Hobkin, Indians—but they were too busy dancing to see her, and Kay was shaking her awake.

"Wha—?" She could still hear the singing.

"Shh!" Kay put her finger on Liza's lips, gesturing toward the window with her head. The moon was a few days from full, and light lay on the floor, marked with the shadows of the open windows. Kay and Liza crawled across the floor to look into the yard.

The grass was white with moonlight where it did not leap with shadow. Enid and Mavis danced with a figure that didn't come up to their chins yet leaped and somersaulted higher than their heads. The owl ducked and darted above. Only on the third repetition did Liza pick any words out of the song's thick accent.

"No more milk to pay my fee,
But Hobkin, Hobkin, Hobkin's free!"

Before she could grasp any more than that, he
leaped up—straight up—swarmed up the windmill,
the outline of his gimme cap thrust against the stars,
reached the top, and kept climbing. Beside her,
Kay grunted in surprise; Liza herself could make no
sound. Up he went, up and up, climbing air and moonlight till the owl swooped below him, and he leaped,
with a laugh, to the owl's back. The bird sneezed once,
circled the yard, and flew away toward the bonfire
field.

Forgetting her bare feet, Liza ran out; but they
had already disappeared. "You get back in here!"
called Kay.

"We've got to catch the goats!" protested Liza, reminded by Mavis skipping happily up to her and tast-
ing her nightgown.

"Okay, but do it in shoes. And don't wake Mom."

Together they rounded up and repenned the goats.
"Did you see him?" asked Liza, torn between the wonder of the sight and the hard knowledge that he had
been glad to go. "Where do you think he's going?"

"Wherever he wants to be, I guess," said Kay slowly,
shutting the pen.

Liza craned back, hoping to see Hobkin and the owl
silhouetted against the moon. "I wish he wasn't gone."

"Then you shouldn't've put out the clothes for him,

should you?" Kay put her arms around Liza. "I'm sorry I didn't believe in him."

Liza leaned against her. "I guess you couldn't help it."

"You okay?"

"I guess so." That wasn't good enough. "Yeah. It kind of hurts my feelings that he wanted to go away, but I don't need him. Not like Aunt Enid did. And it's mean to keep him if he wants to be somewhere else."

But it still hurt, a little bit, to get up the next morning with no smell of coffee in the air and to find the plate and bowl on the back step, unwashed.